# The Trials and Tribulations of a
# Trailer Trash Housewife

## A PLAY IN THREE ACTS

by Del Shores

Music by
Joe Patrick Ward

Lyrics by
Sharyn Lane, Del Shores and
Joe Patrick Ward

SAMUEL FRENCH

FOUNDED 1830

NEW YORK HOLLYWOOD LONDON TORONTO

SAMUELFRENCH.COM

ISBN 978-0-573-66372-7          Printed in U.S.A.          #22820

**IMPORTANT BILLING AND CREDIT
REQUIREMENTS**

All producers of *THE TRIALS AND TRIBULATIONS OF A TRAILER TRASH HOUSEWIFE must* give credit to the Author of the Play in all programs distributed in connection with performances of the Play, and in all instances in which the title of the Play appears for the purposes of advertising, publicizing or otherwise exploiting the Play and/or a production. The name of the Author *must* appear on a separate line on which no other name appears, immediately following the title and *must* appear in size of type not less than fifty percent of the size of the title type.

THE TRIALS AND TRIBULATIONS OF
A TRAILER TRASH HOUSEWIFE
A Play in Three Acts
By
Del Shores
Music by Joe Patrick Ward, Lyrics by Sharyn Lane, Del Shores and
Joe Patrick Ward

***THE TRIALS AND TRIBULATIONS OF A TRAILER TRASH HOUSEWIFE*** was originally produced by Sharyn Lane for The Zephyr Theatre in Hollywood, California, March 8, 2003. It was directed by Del Shores; the music was by Joe Patrick Ward; the lyrics were by Sharyn Lane, Del Shores and Joe Patrick Ward; the musical director was Joe Patrick Ward. The set was by Robert Steinberg; the lights were by Kathi O'Donohue; the sound was by Drew Dalzell; the costume design was by Craig Taggart. The associate producer was Marlana Hope; the production stage manager was John Hagen; the assistant stage managers were Chris Pudlo, Erin Rae and Erin Schlabach. The publicist was Ed Baran; photography was by Rosemary Alexander; website design was by Jason Dottley. Linda Toliver and Gary Guidinger were the artistic directors for the Zephyr Theatre. The cast, in order of appearance, was as follows:

**BLUES SINGER** . . . . . . . . . . . . . . . . . . . . . . . . . . . . . . . . . Debby Holiday

**J.D. WINKLER** . . . . . . . . . . . . . . . . . . . . . . . . . . . . . . . . . . . David Steen

**WILLADEAN WINKLER** . . . . . . . . . . . . . . . . . . . . . . . . . . . . . Beth Grant

**RAYLEEN HOBBS** . . . . . . . . . . . . . . . . . . . . . . . . . . . . . . . . . Dale Dickey

**LA SONIA ROBINSON** . . . . . . . . . . . . . . . . . . . . . . . . . . . Octavia Spencer

Also important and appreciated appearances during the run were: Blake Gibbons (J.D.), Susan Leslie (Rayleen), Angela Teek (Blues Singer), Jennifer Toffell (Willadean) and Pam Trotter (LaSonia and Blues Singer)

Talk Show Voices were: Newell Alexander, Rosemary Alexander, Terry Brannon, Susan Leslie, Jennifer Toffell and Rolanda Watts.

Special thanks to Jason Dottley, our uncredited hero.

# THE CAST

**BLUES SINGER** – 30s, African-American. Sexy and beautiful with a powerful voice.

**J.D. WINKLER** – around 50. Once the handsome quarterback, now the failed, angry, abusive, adulterous, alcoholic husband.

**WILLADEAN WINKLER** – mid- to late 40s. The trapped, weathered and abused housewife who has a beautiful heart and soul.

**RAYLEEN HOBBS** – late 30s. The much-married waitress with the great body, the hard, lived-in face who desperately needs acceptance.

**LA SONIA ROBINSON** – late 30s, African-American. Willadean's fleshy neighbor and best friend who speaks her mind and has little fear.

A pianist also appears onstage who accompanies the Blue Singer.

# THE SETTINGS

A small trailer house; a bar called The Spotlight; the entrance to a Super Wal-Mart (accomplished through lighting).

# THE TIME

Three days in the summer of 2005.

# AUTHOR'S NOTE

To strive for the truth, I did massive research into the psychology of the victims and the abusers of domestic violence. Actors and directors, I challenge you to do the same. What unlocked the Winklers for me was linked to the sexuality of the couple. Why does Willadean stay? Why do so many women continue "the sick dance" of provoking, engaging, which inevitably leads to abuse? Because in the cycle, there is the making up, the "I'm sorry" which almost always leads to affection, sex and feeling loved.

Regarding the use of guns in this production, please be responsible and get a professional to assist you for complete safety. The fighting should look real, but the actors should again feel and be completely safe. A fight choreographer is recommended.

# ACT ONE

*(In darkness, we hear the blues, piano style. Red bar room lights are slowly brought up on a beautiful* **BLUES SINGER** *draped across the piano. She is dressed to the nines, in a red slinky gown, slit up to her ass, a red boa and a red flower in her hair. She taps her fingers to the beat.* **THE PIANIST**, *dressed in a dark suit, hits a chord and our beautiful, powerful* **BLUES SINGER** *sings "The Trailer Trash Blues.")*

**BLUES SINGER.**

I've had trials and tribulations.

And I've had lost expectations.

I've been low-down and put down

And beat down and dismissed.

Yes, I have.

But lately I've been thinkin'

Sometimes when I've been drinkin'.

There just ain't no forgivin'

This here stinkin' life I'm livin'.

No, I want…

Oh, I want much more than this.

*(She slides off the piano, then stands by the piano as lights are brought up across the stage in the trailer court as* **WILLADEAN** *(**WILLI**)* **WINKLER**, *mid- to late- forties, weathered, lived-in face, rushes into her trailer house, carrying a bag of groceries, pausing at the door. NOTE: The name "**LA SONIA**" is pronounced like the pasta dish "Lasagna.")*

**WILLI.** *(yelling)* LaSonia! I'm home! They've got on Strippers for Jesus today. Hurry!

*(She rushes into her trailer home, starts unpacking her groceries as the* **BLUES SINGER** *slaps the top of the piano and sings:)*

**BLUES SINGER.**

I got those

Trailer Trash Blues.

There are sisters out there

Who understand me.

*(spoken to audience member)* Yeah, you hear me talkin' to you.

*(In the kitchen area of the trailer,* **WILLI** *opens a can of peaches, puts them in two bowls, adds whipped cream on top, places them into the refrigerator, then takes a tuna casserole out of the refrigerator.)*

Mm-hm, these sisters,

They got misters

That won't let 'em be.

*(spoken to* **WILLI***)* You listenin' to me?!

*(Lights are brought up more in the bar area to reveal* **J.D. WINKLER**, *a stud of a fifty year-old man, sitting at a table, surrounded by about six empty beer bottles.)*

Seems your man's always pickin' a fight.

He says nothin' that you do is right.

You take his abuse.

And what's your excuse?

"I love him, I love him!"

Yeah, right.

Maybe it's because you know

You've got nowhere else to go.

*(She walks over to* **WILLI***.)*

Sad little housewife,

Stuck in a trailer all day...

*(***WILLI** *glances at the clock on the wall, then goes to the door, opens it.)*

**WILLI.** *(calling)* LaSonia! C'mon, hurry!

**BLUES SINGER.**
While her husband is off in some beer joint
Drinkin' away.

**J.D.** Hey! Any way I get a beer *today*?!

(**RAYLEEN HOBBS**, *the 40ish, trashy waitress here – everything she wears is too tight – enters the bar from a back entrance carrying a case of beer.*)

**RAYLEEN.** Okay, okay! Damn, hell, shit, fuck!

(**RAYLEEN** *drops the case of beer on the bar, then grabs a fresh beer for* **J.D.** *and slams it on the table in front of him.* **J.D.** *stares at her ass while* **RAYLEEN** *clears the empty bottles from his table. She then moves to the bar, tossing bottles, cleaning ashtrays and wiping it down.*)

**BLUES SINGER.**
Wife is cookin' supper,
As if it would matter.
Her louse of a spouse
Will prob'ly throw it right at her.
So much for supper.
Flushed down the bowl.
Waste of a good casserole!

**WILLI.** *(yelling out door)* LaSonia, five minutes! I got the popcorn on.

(**WILLI** *throws a bag of popcorn into the microwave and pops it.*)

**BLUES SINGER.**
That poor gal,
She's brokenhearted.
She feels lonesome and discarded,
And distressed and distraught and disgraced
And discouraged as hell.
*(with a glance to* **WILLI***)* You can tell.

(**BLUES SINGER** *picks up remote, mimes turning on TV, lounges on the sofa.*)

**BLUES SINGER.** *(Cont.)*

Leads a life so ordinary

That it's almost kinda scary.

On her sofa, there she'll linger

Watching Oprah, Jerry Springer

And Montel.

Oh…

And Sally Jesse Rafael.

*(spoken)* Before they canceled her ass.

**WILLI.** *(opens door, yells)* LaSonia! Get a move on, girl! Judge Judy's nearly over!

*(The* **BLUES SINGER** *climbs up on* **WILLI***'s coffee table, performs full out.)*

**BLUES SINGER.**

Got those Trailer Trash Blues!

When the kids are long gone,

You got nothin'.

Nothin' at all,

Except a husband

Who is hateful, ungrateful and mean…

Like you never seen!

Maybe sometimes he'll throw you a bone.

Guess it's better than bein' alone.

What's yours is now his.

The worst of it is

You've still got some dreams of your own.

*(Music stops.* **WILLI** *grabs a dictionary from the book shelf, sits at the table, opens it, closes her eyes and points.)*

**WILLI.** *(reading)* "Stuck." Well, I already know that one.

*(The* **BLUES SINGER** *shakes her head. Then continues singing.)*

**BLUES SINGER.**

Just forget all aspirations.

Your life is now one of frustrations.
Of grief and woe and complications.
Of many trials and tribulations…
When you've got those
Trailer Trash Blues.

*(The* **PIANIST** *"rolls" a crescendoed chord underneath her last note, as they end with a flourish. The* **BLUES SINGER** *and the* **PIANIST** *exit. Lights are lowered in the bar.* **J.D.** *continues to drink and stare at* **RAYLEEN***, who has settled at the bar, doing puzzles from a puzzle book. Full lights are brought up in the trailer house as* **WILLI** *closes the dictionary, then reopens it.)*

**WILLI.** *(reading)* "Pulverize: To grind or be ground into powder." Hmm, let's see. I pulverized the corn and made corn meal. That seems right. *(She suddenly has a panic attack; mutters.)* I'm not gonna shrivel up and die, I'm not gonna to shrivel up and die. I'm not gonna shrivel up and die. *(She takes several deep breaths, then looks up at the clock, runs to the door, opens it and yells.)* LaSonia, it's startin'! *(She puts the dictionary back in the bookshelf.)* Pulverize. The Indians pulverized red clay and made war paint. Ooh, that's good usage. *(calmer)* I am not gonna shrivel up and die.

*(She moves to the living room area, finds the remote and turns on the TV.)*

**STRIPPER VOICE.** *(on TV)* I have won twenty-seven souls to Jesus while lap dancing.

**WILLI.** Where is she? *(She rushes to the back door, opens it and yells.)* LaSonia! LaSonia! Hurry! One's wearin' a cross *and* a corset, I kid you not.

**STRIPPER VOICE.** *(on TV)* My mama actually got me started in the strippin' business. We used to have a mother-daughter act called The Jugs. But Mama got emphysema. A smoker. She'd have coughin' fits during our act which was very disturbing to the customers, so she had to quit. Heartbreakin'.

**LA SONIA.** *(O.S., overlaps TV)* Willi, I'm comin', I'm comin'!

*(LA SONIA ROBINSON enters. She is WILLI's next door neighbor, late 30's. A fleshy African American, who has little fear and speaks her mind.)*

**LA SONIA.** *(overlaps TV)* I'm sorry. I was on the internet and lost track of time.

**WILLI.** You and that internet.

*(WILLI takes the popped corn out of the microwave and pours it in a bowl. The two friends move to the couch, a routine they are both very familiar with. The popcorn sits between them and they eat while they watch.)*

**LA SONIA.** I brung you the new "O." It has that article about "How To Talk To Yourself Nicely."

*(LA SONIA puts the magazine on the coffee table.)*

**WILLI.** Oh, I need that. Hush up now.

**LA SONIA.** Sorry.

**TALK SHOW HOST.** *(on TV)* So, your employer doesn't mind? The witnessing for Jesus, testifying for the Lord, while you are on the job?

**STRIPPER VOICE.** *(on TV)* Oh, no. I won him to the Lord, too. And if Jesus can save a strip club owner, he can save anyone.

**LA SONIA.** She got a point.

**WILLI.** Indeed she does.

**TALK SHOW HOST.** *(on TV)* Next up we have some of Misty's customers to talk about their conversion experiences. We'll be right back.

*(Music, then LA SONIA hits the mute button. WILLI gets up, pulls the casserole out of the oven as LA SONIA thumbs through the magazine.)*

**WILLI.** I see that waitress that moved into space seventeen has put out a bunch of little gnomes.

**LA SONIA.** Nasty ugly things. Give me the heebie jeebies. Brings down the whole neighborhood along with that poor excuse for a trailer. She livin' in a camper shell!

**WILLI.** I know it. There used to be rules about no travel trailers in this court and such things but they lowered their standards – right before you moved in. *(WILLI holds a spoonful of casserole out to* **LA SONIA**.) Taste this. She is a curious one. There's a story there, I guarantee you. Does it need anything else?

**LA SONIA.** A little more salt. Did you use garlic powder?

**WILLI.** Uh-huh. Thought I'd try somethin' different.

**LA SONIA.** Well, she is trash that will not burn. That's all I know.

**WILLI.** LaSonia, now be nice.

**LA SONIA.** Have you seen the way she dresses? Cut off jeans and tube tops. At her age. And white! Now *that* is white. I don't believe she owns a mirror, otherwise she would not go out of the house lookin' like that.

**WILLI.** Well, bless her heart. I suspect a lot of heartache in that girl. I see it in her eyes. She has those sad pitiful eyes. All it needs is the Lays Potato Chips. I usually wait 'til I hear J.D. drive up, then I crunch 'em up, put it in the oven and supper's on the table in ten minutes. J.D. does not like to wait for his supper.

**LA SONIA.** Well, ain't you just the regular Martha Stewart. Although I don't think Martha would ever make a tuna casserole.

**WILLI.** She might have when she was in prison. I bet her fellow inmates would've liked it better than that nasty ol' prison food.

**LA SONIA.** *(laughing)* Go on, girl.

**WILLI.** I tried the Baked Lays once.

**LA SONIA.** Baked Lays?

**WILLI.** When I went on that health kick –

**LA SONIA.** Baked Lays ain't right.

**WILLI.** It wadn't bad – but J.D. got so mad he threw the entire casserole out the back door.

**LA SONIA.** I remember. I stepped in it. I thought J.D. had got drunk and tossed his cookies.

**WILLI.** Oh, J.D. never vomits when he's drunk. He's a professional drunk. *(They share a laugh.)* She's working as a waitress at the Spotlight – number seventeen. Rayleen Hobbs.

**LA SONIA.** White trash name.

**WILLI.** I made her some of my cherry dump delight. Even though her spirit is sad, she seems nice. I agree, a little on the trashy side.

**LA SONIA.** A little? Well, I ain't givin' her diddly squat. No ma'am, not going to be neighborly. She is not someone I want to know. You can't just welcome every piece of riff-raft that arrives in this trailer court in with open arms. It will bite you in the ass.

**WILLI.** I was not brought up to ignore my neighbors, LaSonia. I just won't do it.

**LA SONIA.** Anybody who wears tube tops at her age with her white white ass hangin' out of cut-off jeans is nobody I want to know. And those gnomes is unsightly.

**WILLI.** She's been collectin' them for years.

**LA SONIA.** Why? They ugly!

**WILLI.** You're too judgmental, LaSonia. God loves all creatures, you know that.

**LA SONIA.** I bet he got to work overtime on that one.

**WILLI.** Well, I see your point. She does use the "F" word an awful lot even when she's not mad. Never heard anything like it in my life.

**LA SONIA.** Bar trash. Worse kind of trash.

**WILLI.** Except circus trash. Thiefs.

**LA SONIA.** And don't get me started on carnival trash.

**WILLI.** Un-uh.

**LA SONIA.** All those freaks and little midgets runnin' around. They scare me. Just like gnomes. *(notices TV)* Ooh, come quick, come quick. They's gettin' all riled up. We just might get some hair pullin' today!

*(WILLI rushes over and sits as LA SONIA punches the remote.)*

**REDNECK VOICE.** *(on TV)* And I sure as hell don't want to go to a strip club and hear about Jesus! If I wanted to hear about Jesus, I'd go to church.

**WILLI.** I agree. Hearin' about Jesus while watchin' someone strip just has to be a little bit off-puttin'.

**STRIPPER VOICE.** *(on TV)* Jesus is everywhere, my friend.

**REDNECK VOICE.** *(on TV)* I don't see him here today. Nope not here. Jesus, if you are here, stand up.

*(POP! The TV sputters and goes black.)*

**WILLI.** Well, what in the world?

**LA SONIA.** No!

**WILLI.** Oh no, this can't be.

**(WILLI** *punches the remote over and over, then rushes over and frantically pushes the buttons on the TV. She then hits the TV, unplugs it, plugs it back in. Nothing.)*

**WILLI.** If this is broke, J.D.'s gonna kill me. His game's tonight.

**LA SONIA.** You wanna come over and watch the rest of the show at my trailer?

**WILLI.** Huh?

**LA SONIA.** You wanna come over and watch the rest of the program at my place?

**WILLI.** No. Nuh-un. Dang it all. Why did this have to happen? You go on. Tell me how it turns out. I'm gonna see if I can get this to work.

**LA SONIA.** You a TV repair man now?

**WILLI.** J.D.'s game's tonight. Oh God, why did this have to happen – ?

**LA SONIA.** It's an old TV. You didn't break it. He shouldn't be mad at you over an old TV breakin'.

**WILLI.** Well, he will not be happy.

**LA SONIA.** Now Willi, this time you cover your face if he starts in on you.

**WILLI.** LaSonia, you know he never really hits me.

**LA SONIA.** Bull – shit! Who you talkin' to? Huh? That's exactly what my sister used to say. I've known you for five years now and I hear what I hear.

**WILLI.** LaSonia, please. I need to fix this TV.

**LA SONIA.** One day my sister came over with a black eye and a busted lip and she tried to tell me –

**WILLI.** *(close to tears)* LaSonia! Please! I don't want to hear about your sister. Not today. I love you, but pretty please with sugar on top. I need to fix this TV –

**LA SONIA.** You don't never want to hear about my sister because if you did, it –

**WILLI.** LaSonia, honey, I cannot hear about your sister today. I'll hear about your sister another day –

**LA SONIA.** That's what you always say –

**WILLI.** I really need to fix this TV, okay? So, please just go home and let me –

**LA SONIA.** Okay. I'm sorry. I –

**WILLI.** I know how to handle my husband. I've been handling my own husband for a long time –

**LA SONIA.** Hmph — !

**WILLI.** I'm gonna be fine. I just need to fix this TV –

**LA SONIA.** Okay. I was just tryin' to –

**WILLI.** *(exploding)* What you're tryin' is my patience!

**LA SONIA.** I'm sorry.

**WILLI.** *(pause, realization)* I'm sorry. Now could we please stop all this negativity. Remember what Dr. Phil says. "What you believe you can achieve." Well, I believe I can fix that television before J.D. gets home and everything is gonna turn out A-okay. Bye-bye.

*(She ushers* **LA SONIA** *out. Pause. Pause.* **LA SONIA** *flies back in.)*

**LA SONIA.** Dr. Phil's full of shit.

**WILLI.** Oh, for cryin' out loud!

**LA SONIA.** You ain't fixin' that TV. Dr. Phil wadn't talkin' about your TV. Fixin' that TV ain't realistic.

**WILLI.** He mighta been. Now go on home. I'll see ya tomorrow.

**LA SONIA.** Yes you will…*(exits, trails off, O.S.)*…but Dr. Phil's full of shit.

*(***WILLI** *stares at the TV, then goes and looks at the back of it. She rushes into the kitchen, opens a drawer and grabs a screw driver, a pair of pliers and a hammer. She begins to unscrew the back of the set while lights come up in the bar.* **J.D.** *calls over to* **RAYLEEN.***)*

**J.D.** Hey, you. Over here. Shake a tail-feather.

**RAYLEEN.** The name is Rayleen. Rayleen Hobbs. Maybe if you call me by my name instead of "Hey" like you was in a barnyard somewhere, I'd rush over with a beer.

**J.D.** Hey! Rayleen Hobbs. Wiggle your cute little ass over here with a cold 'un.

**RAYLEEN.** That's more like it.

**J.D.** And a bag of Fritos – Rayleen Hobbs.

**RAYLEEN.** *(smiling and flirting)* That's even more like it.

**J.D.** You live in our trailer court, don't ya?

**RAYLEEN.** Right across the way in my little bit of a home. Number seventeen.

**J.D.** You like it here in Mesquite?

**RAYLEEN.** So far, so good. I met your wife. She seems real sweet.

**J.D.** Uh-huh.

**RAYLEEN.** Do y'all have a happy marriage?

**J.D.** What do you think? *(He smiles a seductive smile.)*

**WILLI.** *(fighting a panic attack, muttering)* I'm not gonna shrivel up and die. What you believe you can achieve.

**RAYLEEN.** *(overlap)* I *believe* you are someone I should stay away from.

**J.D.** Then why don't ya?

**RAYLEEN.** Because I work here and I'm doing my job.

*(She sits at the table with **J.D.**)*

**J.D.** Does your job entail sittin' down with the customers shootin' the shit?

**RAYLEEN.** For your information, the state of Texas gives me two fifteen minutes breaks for every eight hour shift.

**J.D.** I see. Well, then, I'm gonna ask you again. On your state of Texas fifteen minute break – why don't you stay away from me?

*(He puts his hand on her leg.)*

**RAYLEEN.** You're askin' me trick questions.

**J.D.** Ain't nothin' trick about the question I'm askin'. So?

**RAYLEEN.** (*laughs*) I can't remember what the question was.

**J.D.** That's probably for the better. So, you ain't married?

**RAYLEEN.** Not no more. I was once. Well, twice. Well five times actually. Things didn't work out. All five times. And there's this law in the state of Texas that says you can't remarry after five times. You'd have to move to another state to get married again. And God, I love Texas. Mesquite trees, hot summers, big hair, big butts…ever'thang. You gotta stop at some point. Gettin' married. My sister told me that. Her friend works for a lawyer. I hate my sister. She's got money now because she married some mucky-muck who works for Exxon – has a big expense account and everything. Lives in Marfa. She's Baptist. Don't get me started on the Baptists. It's just too early. You look up the word "self-righteous" in the dictionary, you'll see her picture.

(*She laughs;* **J.D.** *just stares at her.*)

(**WILLI** *looks at the clock and realizes the time. She leans the back of the TV against it and pockets the screws and screw driver, then rushes over, puts the dictionary in the bookshelf and finishes her casserole.*)

So I just stopped. Marrying. Probably for the best because I seem to be attracted to losers.

**J.D.** Well, for *your* information, I am a winner.

**RAYLEEN.** A winner, huh?

**J.D.** That's right.

**RAYLEEN.** You're married, trying to pick me up. You ain't no winner.

**J.D.** Not happily married. Shit! I stay so horny, the crack of dawn ain't safe. Lotta me to go around. Besides, you been married five times.

**RAYLEEN.** I said I pick losers. It's a pattern of mine.

**J.D.** So all your marriages broke up because of *them*, right? All them shitty men.

**RAYLEEN.** That's right.

**J.D.** That you chose.

**RAYLEEN.** I picked losers. I already been over this with you.

**J.D.** Maybe it's them that picked the loser, Miss five-times-married-cocktail-waitress.

**RAYLEEN.** *(stung, pause)* You know what? You're an asshole.

**J.D.** And you know exactly what you are, don't ya?

**RAYLEEN.** *(gets up)* Fuck you!

**J.D.** In the not too distant future, it'll be my extreme pleasure.

**RAYLEEN.** In your dreams, asswipe. Fuck you!

*(Piano cue as **RAYLEEN** grabs the bag of Fritos and crunches them as **WILLI** in the trailer crunches the potato chips simultaneously. In the bar, **J.D.** throws his head back and laughs, then picks up the bag and pours the crumbs in his mouth. **WILLI** returns to the TV, getting more and more panicked.)*

*(The **BLUES SINGER** enters and sings the reprise to "The Trailer Trash Blues.")*

**BLUES SINGER.**

Always those trials and tribulations.

A life ever fraught with aggravations.

And you keep mopin' and copin'

And hopin' you ain't gonna die.

**WILLI.** I'm not gonna shrivel up and die. I am *not* gonna shrivel up and die.

**BLUES SINGER.**

Just a housewife who's payin' her dues.

Who keeps singin' those Trailer Trash Blues.

Your man's free to roam,

And when he comes home,

You pray that he won't blow a fuse.

**WILLI.** *(mutters)* Must've blown a fuse.

*(**J.D.** finishes his beer in the bar, **RAYLEEN** glares at him, pissed. **WILLI** goes over, takes the back off the TV again and stares hopelessly. She bangs on it in frustration. **J.D.** gets up from the table, goes over to **RAYLEEN**. He stares at her, then pushes her against the bar reaching under her*

*skirt and feeling. She starts to resist, then goes with it.)*

*(**NOTE:** In the original production, during songs, many powerful mirrored movements between* **WILLI** *and* **RAY-LEEN** *were directed and choreographed.)*

**BLUES SINGER.**
> Your self-esteem just keeps on shrinkin'.
> It's "sink or swim," and you are sinkin'.
> Girl, listen up,
> What are you thinkin'?

**WILLI.** I think everything's gonna be all right.

> *(**J.D.** throws down some change and exits. **RAYLEEN**, confused, picks it up and exits. The **BLUES SINGER** exits. A flow to all the exits. **WILLI** continues to set the table, then hears a truck drive up in back of the trailer. She frantically tries to replace the back of the TV set, ultimately just props it against the back of the TV. She sees the "O" magazine on the coffee table, gasps, hides it under the table, throws the leftover popcorn in the trash. She then rushes over and quickly spreads the Lays Potato Chips over the casserole, pops it in the oven, sets the timer, takes out her ponytail, shakes out her hair to look prettier as **J.D.** enters the back door. **WILLI** eyes the TV nervously during:)*

Hey, hon. How was your day?

> *(**J.D.** sets his lunchbox in the sink.)*

**J.D.** Huh? What?

> *(He exits down the hall.)*

**WILLI.** *(calling)* How was your day?

**J.D.** *(O.S.)* Shitty.

**WILLI.** I'm sorry.

**J.D.** *(O.S.)* What?

**WILLI.** I'm sorry that your day was bad.

> *(**J.D.** reenters wearing a white wife-beater tank.)*

**J.D.** My day was shitty, not bad. Damn, woman, shitty is a good word, what's your problem?

**WILLI.** It's vulgar, hon and I don't like usin' it but you are welcome to use salty language, but I don't care to.

**J.D.** *(imitating)* "You are welcome to use salty language, but I don't care to." Hush up, would ya? You're making my day shittier.

**WILLI.** I'm sorry.

**J.D.** And stop being sorry for ever' goddamn thing. What's for supper?

*(She comes over and starts rubbing his back.)*

**WILLI.** *(proud)* Tuna casserole, green beans, Wonder Bread – real fresh, not day old –

**J.D.** A little to the left.

**WILLI.** And yella cling peaches in syrup for dessert from Del Monte.

**J.D.** Right there. There's a knot right there.

*(**WILLI** works on the knot.)*

**WILLI.** It'll all be ready in about *(looks at timer)* seven minutes. Would you like a glass of ice tea while we wait? I think I'm havin' one.

**J.D.** Beer.

**WILLI.** Okay. I'll get you that beer. *(goes to refrigerator, gets beer and opens it)* Did you meet Rayleen yet? I'm sure you did, she's workin' over at the Spotlight for about a week now. She lives right over there in number seventeen with all those little gnomes around. *(hands him beer)* Here ya go. A little shell of a camper thing – about as big as a matchbox– the kind they used to not let in the court – and she drives an old El Camino. She seemed real nice. Sad eyes though. I took her over my cherry dump delight. Woke 'er up because she works 'til two a.m. and doesn't get home 'til around three. Still had make-up on, all smeared. Not a pretty sight, I'm here to tell ya, bless her heart.

**J.D.** You made her cherry dump delight and we're havin' cling peaches for dessert?

**WILLI.** In syrup. I was just tryin' to be neighborly. She seems real nice. Cusses a lot. Uses the "F" word, even when she's not mad. Never heard a woman use the "F" word like that. And hon, you love cling peaches in heavy syrup. Del Monte makes the best.

**J.D.** I like cherry dump delight better. Make me some cherry dump delight tomorrow. And I don't want you being neighborly anymore with that tramp. She's beneath us. When was the last time you made me a steak?

**WILLI.** Steak night is the third Wednesday of the month. That's all we can afford, J.D. I do my best.

**J.D.** You clippin' coupons? Lookin' for specials? Don't steak ever go on special?

**WILLI.** I buy it on special. I do my very best.

(**J.D.** *goes over and slaps* **WILLI** *on her ass. She smiles, likes it.*)

**J.D.** Your very best is flat out shitty if you ask me. Always has been. You better start comin' up with some more ideas on how I can eat steak more than onced a month. What the hell else do you have to do around here? Huh? Start thinking how you can make me steak more than once a month. You ain't retarded.

**WILLI.** Okay, I will. Oh, I have an idea. Why don't you give me sixty dollars a week instead of fifty-five. I could get you steak twice a month then. Maybe three times if I can find good specials.

**J.D.** I can't afford that and you know it. That's a shitty idea.

**WILLI.** (*very cautious*) Maybe if you came home here and had your beers – here – instead of at The Spotlight, we could, well afford it. Steak. I've been thinkin' J.D. Maybe you could cut down there to once or twice a week and you could have your after-work beers here and we could go to a movie on dollar night and I could get steak more often. Wouldn't that be nice?

**J.D.** No, it would *not* be nice. I work my ass off for us and you are trying to take away my one true pleasure in life. Winding down with a beer after work at The Spotlight.

**WILLI.** Now J.D., I suspect you have more than one beer.

(**J.D.** *slams down his beer on the coffee table, gets up and goes towards her. He pushes his crotch up against her leg, then puts his face against hers – then suddenly grabs* *a handful of hair and pulls.)*

**J.D.** Say you're sorry. Say your sorry for trying to take away my one true pleasure in life. Say you're sorry Willadean for trying to take your hardworkin' husband's one true pleasure away. Say it!

**WILLI.** *(in pain)* I'm sorry.

(**J.D.** *pulls her hair harder.)*

**J.D.** For trying to take away the one true pleasure from my hardworkin' husband.

**WILLI.** *(overlap, repeating)* I'm sorry I was tryin' to take away the one true pleasure from my hardworkin' husband.

**J.D.** You're sorry all right. You sorry ungrateful ingrate. *(He pushes her as he releases her, then starts pacing.)* You think I like haulin' asphalt from Mesquite to Tyler and back again, then to Denton and back again, then to Plano and back again, then to McKinney and back again, then to Arlington and back again? You think I like my shitty-ass job, Willadean?

**WILLI.** *(looking down)* No –

**J.D.** *(bangs counter)* Look at me when I'm talkin' to you, woman! The only thing I have to look forward to ever' day is gettin' off work and havin' a couple of beers at the Spotlight to *unwind* before I have to come home to *you.* You don't understand stress woman. That's your problem. You don't know what it's like to live with failed dreams ever' day of your life. If you hadn't got pregnant with that little worthless no-count faggot, I coulda played for the Dallas Cowboys. I coulda been Roger fuckin' Stalback, Troy fuckin' Aikman if you hadn't got knocked up to trap me. I was all-district four years in a row! You just don't get it.

**WILLI.** I had dreams too. I have my own dreams.

**J.D.** Bullfuckin'shit! You didn't have no dreams! Now just shut up and get your shitty tuna casserole out of the shitty oven and let's just eat another shitty meal.

*(She hesitates.)*

C'mon!

(**WILLI** *scurries to get the casserole out of the oven, nervously proceeds to serve it, along with the bread and green beans. The silence during the time it takes her to serve him is deadly.* **J.D.** *sits and downs his beer. More silence.* **WILLI** *sits and closes her eyes, folds her hands and prays, mouth moving.* **J.D.** *smirks and shakes his head.*)

**WILLI.** Amen.

(**J.D.** *downs the beer during her prayer, then throws the beer bottle in the trash on "Amen."* **WILLI** *flinches.*)

**J.D.** *(shit-eating grin, charming)* I hope you was prayin' for steak to go on special. *(pause)* Oh, come on, laugh. I made a funny. That's what your problem is. You ain't got no sense of humor.

**WILLI.** I do too have a sense of humor.

**J.D.** Then prove it. Laugh at my funny. I'm gonna say it again.

(*He reaches under the table and grabs her upper thigh, squeezes.*)

**WILLI.** Okay.

**J.D.** I hope you was prayin' for rib-eye steak to go on special.

(**WILLI** *fakes a laugh, or is it real?*)

**WILLI.** Oh, that's funny, J.D.

**J.D.** So was you?

**WILLI.** Was I what?

**J.D.** Prayin' for steak to go on special?

**WILLI.** No.

**J.D.** Why not? That's a good prayer.

**WILLI.** Because I think God has better things to do than to arrange for steak to go on special down at the Super Wal-Mart.

**J.D.** So, what was you prayin' for? World peace?

**WILLI.** No.

**J.D.** Then what?

**WILLI.** *(pause, then softly)* Just peace. Just plain ol' peace. I'll make you cherry dump delight for dessert tomorrow.

*(She feels his leg with her bare foot under the table.)*

**J.D.** That's my girl. Oh shoot, the game.

*(**WILLI** flinches as **J.D.** walks over to pick up the remote control.)*

**WILLI.** *(panicked)* J.D., while I was watching –

**J.D.** Hold on, hold on, hold on. Where's the remote?

**WILLI.** J.D. –

**J.D.** Here it is. *(click, nothing)* What the hell's wrong with the TV?

*(He walks over to the set and sees the disassembled back. **NOTE:** The following should have an overlap effect, lines spewing, no pauses.)*

**WILLI.** J.D., today while I was watching –

**J.D.** What the hell happened to the television, Willadean – ?

**WILLI.** I'm sorry. While I was watchin'…I didn't do anything, it just popped —

**J.D.** Popped? Goddamn you! How the hell am I supposed to watch the goddamn game? Huh? What the hell did you do to it – ?

**WILLI.** Nothin'. It popped and I was trying to fix –

**J.D.** You was tryin' to fix it? You was tryin' to fix it? What the hell do you know about fixin' a broke TV? I want to watch my game and you broke my TV!

**WILLI.** I'm sor –

**J.D.** You broke my TV, Willadean!

*(He kicks the coffee table exposing the hidden "O" Magazine under the coffee table. He snatches it up.)*

What the hell is this? Has that bitch been over here again? I told you I don't want her in my house! You and that goddamn fat-ass have been watching my TV ever' day nonstop and you broke my TV. You tell that bitch that she's not welcome here anymore and she can go find other friends. Her own kind!

*(Exits trailer, throws magazine at **LA SONIA**'s trailer, then storms back in.)*

**J.D.** All you do is sit and do nothin' and watch TV all day and now you broke it! Goddamn it!

**WILLI.** J.D., what am I supposed to do? You get to watch –

**J.D.** You're not supposed to break my TV, that's what your supposed to do. And I don't want you watchin' TV with her in my house ever again!

**WILLI.** She's my only friend –

**J.D.** You get rid of her, I mean it! You don't need no friends. You tell that bitch she's not welcome in this house anymore. I mean it, Willadean. *(storms to door, points)* And don't you even speak to that tramp in number seventeen! I've had it! This is my house and I say what's what and you are forbade to watch TV anymore. Got it? And I want steak more than once a month! 'Cause I'm tired of these fuckin' casseroles. Got it? *(He throws his plate in the garbage.)* And you are paying for fixing that TV. Got it?

**WILLI.** J.D., please stop yellin'. People can hear –

**J.D.** I don't give a shit! You broke my TV! You did this so you could go to dollar movie night, didn't you?

**WILLI.** No, I....

**J.D.** I'll yell if I goddamn want to yell. This is my goddamn trailer house! Bought and paid for by *me*. And you're gonna pay to get that TV fixed!

**WILLI.** How am I supposed to pay for fixin' –

**J.D.** You figure it out! Goddamn you! And it better not affect my steak Wednesday, goddamn it!

**WILLI.** Fine, then I'll get a job!

**J.D.** You will not! No wife of mine is gonna work. You will not get a job! You'll figure another way, but you sure as shit ain't gonna get a job!

**WILLI.** Then how am I supposed to pay for fixin' – ?

**J.D.** You figure it out! You broke my TV and I can't watch my game!

**WILLI.** I'm gonna get a job!

**J.D.** You will not!

**WILLI.** I will so and I'll go to dollar night with LaSonia and you can't stop me – !

**J.D.** The hell I can't! Goddamn you!

*(He rushes her. SLAP, SLAP, SLAP.* **WILLI** *screams as he knocks her to the floor, starts to kick her then stops, goes to the bookshelf for the Bible.* **NOTE:** *The fighting needs to look realistic, although the actors should feel safe. A fight choreographer is recommended.)*

You will not get a goddamn job! *(He pushes the Bible into* **WILLI***'s head.)* "Wives submit yourselves unto your husbands as unto the Lord." Ephesians 5:22. YOU WILL NOT GET A GODDAMN JOB!

*(He then puts the Bible back, then exits down the hall, returning putting on his shirt.)*

Goddamn you, Willi. You caused this.

**WILLI.** Please don't leave.

**J.D.** You broke my TV and caused me to get mad and miss my game and I didn't even get a proper meal. Goddamn you.

*(He exits, she gets up and follows, watches.)*

**WILLI.** Please don't – J.D.!

*(She walks back into the trailer, takes a deep breath.)*

I'm not gonna shrivel up and die. I'm not gonna shrivel up and die. I'm not gonna shrivel up and die.

*(BLACKOUT)*

### End of Act One

### Transition

*(The **PIANIST** plays "Willadean," an instrument bridge. Lights creep up to dimly light the trailer and the bar. In the trailer, **WILLI** cleans up the aftermath. The table is cleared, the sofa put back in place, everything is returned to order. She acknowledges the pain in her arm as she works. In the bar, **RAYLEEN** enters and cleans off the table, the crumbled Fritos off the floor, then wipes down the bar. Some mirroring in movement of **WILLI** and **RAY-LEEN** during their cleaning. **WILLI** pauses and looks around at her existence while **RAYLEEN** sits at the table, lights a cigarette, reflects for a moment. Then, they both exit simultaneously.)*

*(A long pause with the music building.)*

*(Then, **J.D.** stumbles into the trailer, a little drunk, full of regret. He goes and opens the refrigerator, pulls out a beer, but before he opens it, he fixates on **WILLI**'s recipe box. He opens it, thumbs through it and finds what he is looking for – a couple of pictures. He stares at them, allows emotion to creep in, then pushes it away and returns the pictures to their hiding place. The hall light comes on and **WILLI** comes to the doorway. **J.D.** turns and sees her. She opens her arms and he rushes to her. They hug, then she takes his hand and leads him to the bedroom as the music transitions – )*

# ACT TWO

*(Lights come up in the bar, as the MUSIC TRANSI-*
*TIONS, bringing on the* **BLUES SINGER***, who struts in,*
*sits on the bar table and wails "Ode to Womankind" in*
*a short, red sassy dress.)*

**BLUES SINGER.**

Let me sing you a love song.

Nothing mushy or cliché.

It's an Ode to Womankind

That just might bring you peace of mind.

A testament to nature's perfect way.

Our lady friend, the Praying Mantis,

Lures her mate to bed.

She says the sweetest things

And while they're in the heat of things,

Lady fair bites off his head.

*(spoken)* It's getting good now, ain't it.

*(She moves to the kitchen table, sits on it.)*

And in her little hive,

The Queen of Bees

Gives her Romeo her heart.

She calls, he takes the lead

And after they have done the deed,

Queeny rips her boy apart.

*(spoken)* Two bees or not two bees.

*(She struts to the coffee table and sits.)*

*(Lights up in the trailer as* **WILLI** *rushes in, carrying a*
*bag of groceries and a Dr. Phil book. During the song,*
*she unpacks her groceries, pulls out newspaper want ads,*
*and puts them on the coffee table, along with the book.)*

**BLUES SINGER.**

> The Black Widow has it all worked out.
>
> She's the one who's in control.
>
> Spin a web,
>
> Cast a spell,
>
> After makin' whoopee, well…
>
> Girlfriend eats her lover whole!
>
> *(spoken)* And a tasty thing he is!
>
> **(WILLI** *gets her dictionary and settles at the kitchen table.)*
>
> *(The Blues singer struts and brings it on home.)*
>
> Oh, the bugs and the bees
>
> Can teach us all a thing or two.
>
> Wives, you gotta love your man,
>
> But if the shit should hit the fan,
>
> Do unto him
>
> Before he does unto you.
>
> Oh yeah!
>
> *(spoken to* **WILLI***)* Do it, girl!
>
> *(And with that, the* **BLUES SINGER** *exits and lights go out in the bar.)*

**WILLI.** *(reading)* "Pau-ci-ty." Paucity. Let's see…means "Few-ness." "Scarcity." I'll never use that one. Don't need it. It's just too late in life to learn words you don't need. *(flips the page and points)* "Solidarity." "Complete unity, as of opinion, feeling, etc." Hmmm…Women world-wide were in solidarity against their mean husbands. Oh, that is good usage. Solidarity. Solidarity. *(She closes the dictionary, goes and puts it up, then scans the want ads.)* No experience necessary.

**LA SONIA.** *(O.S.)* Willi! Willi, baby! Open up the door! I'm about to drop this TV!

**WILLI.** TV?

> **(WILLI** *rushes over and opens the door and* **LA SONIA** *enters carrying an old portable black and white TV.)*

**LA SONIA.** I found this in the storage shed. You can borrow it 'til you get that 'un fixed.

*(She sets it on top of the old one, plugs it in,* **WILLI** *is concerned.)*

When we got the color set, LaVell said, "Get that ol' thang outta my house, we's in style now with our RCA color TV." Then he started singing the Jeffersons' song. "Movin' on up." That Lavell cracks me up sometimes.

**WILLI.** You're lucky to have him.

**LA SONIA.** You okay?

**WILLI.** Uh-huh. I'm fine. Just trying to figure out my life.

**LA SONIA.** And how's that goin'?

**WILLI.** Better than you'd think.

**LA SONIA.** Where'd you go this morning? I came over to check on you and you was already gone.

**WILLI.** I walked into town. Dr. Phil's book came out on paperback, so I took some of my saved change and bought a copy. Then I went over to the Wash N' Fold and called John David on the pay phone there, listened to his message and told him I loved him. Sat and read my book for a spell then found a newspaper someone left and I read that. I completely lost track of time. When I realized it, I rushed over to the Super Wal-Mart because I had enough money to get J.D. a steak for supper and the ingredients for his cherry dump delight.

**LA SONIA.** *(making a judgment)* Ah, ha. *(pause)* Well, we done missed all our shows.

**WILLI.** I know and I'm sorry, but I just loved getting out of the house, LaSonia. I've decided I need a purpose. There's a whole chapter about it in Dr. Phil's book.

**LA SONIA.** Mm, hmm. Your needin' a purpose done caused us to miss all our shows. Oprah had on Meryl Streep and Olivia Newton-John talking about pesticides and how they cause the cancer in little chi'ren.

*(***WILLI*** picks up the steak, unwraps it.)*

**WILLI.** Well, I'm sorry I missed that one. That sounds real important.

*(***LA SONIA*** stares at the steak; shakes her head.)*

**LA SONIA.** Um, um, um.

**WILLI.** What?

**LA SONIA.** J.D. beat the shit outta of you and you making him steak and and it ain't even the third Wednesday of the month.

**WILLI.** He just pushed me a little, mostly took it out on the dishes. Nothin' I can't handle. Believe me, he came back, woke me up and apologized good and proper.

**LA SONIA.** Um, hum.

(**LA SONIA** *gets up, evaluates* **WILLI**, *sits at the kitchen table.*)

**WILLI.** I thought it might offset him bein' upset over the broke TV. A steak. I just got one. I'll just have leftover tuna casserole. It was a cheap cut so I'm gonna soak it in milk to tenderize it, then I'm gonna pan fry it. Oooh, I better get on that. Look at the time.

(*She goes and puts the groceries up, pours some milk in a bowl, puts the raw steak in it during:*)

**LA SONIA.** You sure you okay?

**WILLI.** I'm fine, I told you. Thank you for being so concerned. You are so sweet. And thank you for the TV. But you can't leave it here. You're gonna have to cart it back and forth because J.D. would not like you loaning me a TV – but I thank you so much. So very much. You are just the very best friend anyone could ever hope for. Isn't life great, LaSonia?!

**LA SONIA.** (*a look*) You been nippin' on the vanilla extracts?

**WILLI.** No. I've just been reading Dr. Phil's book and I have just decided to take his advice and take control of my life and find a purpose.

**LA SONIA.** I told you Dr. Phil's full of shit. The only reason he's anybody is 'cause of Oprah.

**WILLI.** No, he is not, he is a saint! And I'm gonna embrace this life that I've been given and make changes. Positive changes. I am in charge. I am. I'm tired of being the victim, La Sonia. Tired of letting my life run me. I'm now going to run my life. And I'm gonna find myself a purpose!

**LA SONIA.** Well, good luck with all that shit.

*(She gets up, starts circling* **WILLI**, *looking for evidence of the beating.)*

Where'd he hit ya? I don't see where that son-of-a-bitch hit you.

**WILLI.** He didn't hit me.

**LA SONIA.** I know he hit you. I heard you scream. Where'd he hit you? I bet he hit you where nobody can see like that asshole used to do to my sister.

*(***LA SONIA*** lifts up her skirt, ***WILLI*** slaps her hand away, but not before ***LA SONIA*** sees a purple bruise.)*

**WILLI.** Stop that! I told you he didn't hurt me. Mostly took it out on the dishes.

**LA SONIA.** Then why there a big purple bruise on your leg? Did he go down to The Spotlight to get drunker?

**WILLI.** I don't know, LaSonia. But he came back and we made up good and proper. *(turning back, lifting her skirt)* Oh, that's an old bruise I got last week when I got up in the middle of the night to get some water and bumped into the end of the bed.

**LA SONIA.** That ain't the color of no old bruise.

**WILLI.** Oh, I read in the paper they're hirin' part timers over at the Super Wal-Mart. No experience necessary. I'm thinkin' of applyin'.

**LA SONIA.** You what?

**WILLI.** I'm thinkin' of applyin' over at the Super Wal-Mart. That'd give me a purpose.

**LA SONIA.** Workin' at the Wal-Mart gonna give you a purpose?

**WILLI.** That's what I said. You always say that LaVell says it's a great place to work. Ever since I lost my babies, I don't feel I have a purpose, LaSonia. I need a purpose. First John David left. Then Melissa. Gone. They were my purpose. *(looks around)* Where's my purpose anymore? I don't have a purpose and I need a purpose. If I don't find a purpose, I'm gonna shrivel up and die. Dr. Phil says we need a purpose and he also says that what you believe you can achieve. So, I want a job at the Super Wal-Mart.

**LA SONIA.** Well, you didn't fix that TV and you said that you believed you could.

**WILLI.** *(a look, then:)* Sometimes I don't like you.

**LA SONIA.** Oh, but I love you, Willi and I want you to find that purpose, but I heard y'all fightin' and I know the truth. Look at me, baby girl. This is LaSonia you talkin' to. Your big black friend next door with the big ears and big mouth. I heard what he said. He said if you got a job that –

**WILLI.** I don't like you eavesdroppin' on us.

**LA SONIA.** You live in a trailer park! You think I really want to hear your shit?

**WILLI.** I don't want to talk about this –

**LA SONIA.** Because you know LaSonia speak the truth and you lyin' about J.D. beatin' –

**WILLI.** He does not *beat* me! He loses his temper sometimes, pushes me a little –

**LA SONIA.** He beat the shit out of you and if you get a job, he gonna beat you again –

**WILLI.** He did not beat me! He just pushed me a little.

**LA SONIA.** That's what my sister always said, but she winded up –

**WILLI.** LaSonia, you are ruinin' my good day!

**LA SONIA.** You have a big purple bruise on your leg just like my sister –

**WILLI.** I don't want to hear about your sister today and that bruise is old –!!

**LA SONIA.** You don't want to hear about my sister any day because –

**WILLI.** *(exploding)* You act like you know my life and you don't! You don't know what he was like. What he came from. His mean ol' daddy. What he made out of himself. J.D. was the most…Oh God, LaSonia, he was… And he chose me. Me, LaSonia. Ever'body wanted him and he chose me. Me! And he came back last night and loved on me. Hard! You don't know how hard that man can love!

**LA SONIA.** That ain't love. That ain't love a'tall.

**WILLI.** J.D. does love me. I do know he loves me. And he makes me happy.

**LA SONIA.** Then why you lookin' for a purpose?!!!

**WILLI.** I don't know! You are getting me so riled up and –

**LA SONIA.** Because I tell the truth –!!

**WILLI.** Oh God, I'm so mixed up right now. I get so confused about it all. Frustrated. And I'm sorry. I shouldn't lash out at you. You're just tryin' to help. I'm sorry. And I'm mad 'cause you're right. I can't get that job at the Super Wal-Mart. I don't know what I was thinkin'. I just thought that maybe I could find myself a purpose. And I am not happy. I'm miserable. Oh, God, I hate him, LaSonia. I know it's not right to hate, it's such a harsh word, but I can't help it. I love him, then I hate him. I love him, then I hate him! There I said it. I told you the truth.

**LA SONIA.** I *know* the truth, baby girl. You don't have to even tell me. And you *never* have to lie to your buddy, your pal, LaSonia.

*(Silence. **WILLI** stares at her.)*

Did you hear what I just said to you?

**WILLI.** Yes. Thank you.

*(Pause, **LA SONIA** hugs her; **WILLI** breaks down.)*

**LA SONIA.** Let it go, baby.

**WILLI.** Sometimes I hate me more than I hate him. And I get so confused and my soul is tormented. And lately, I've been…I've been havin' these terrible thoughts, LaSonia. Fantasies.

**LA SONIA.** *(breaking the hug)* Fantasies? What kind of fantasies, girl? Come over here and tell me all about these fantasies!

*(She pulls her to the couch. They sit.)*

**WILLI.** I want to pulverize him.

**LA SONIA.** Pulver-what?

**WILLI.** Pul-ver-ize.

**LA SONIA.** That your new word for today?

**WILLI.** Yesterday's. Today's was "solidarity." Pulverize means to grind up into powder. Like pioneers did when they crushed wheat and made flour. Ever since I learned it, I've been havin' fantasies of J.D. being ground up into powder.

**LA SONIA.** And how you gonna grind him up?

**WILLI.** I haven't gotten that far in my fantasies, but I do know I'd like to put him in the palm of my hand and just blow him away...Oh, Lord I gotta stop these thoughts and make supper.

*(She gets up,* **LA SONIA** *reaches up and pulls her back on the couch.)*

**LA SONIA.** Sit yo ass back down! These are good thoughts! Wonderful fantasies. Maybe *this* could be your purpose. Oooh, ooh, maybe you could kill him somehow – feed him Drano or just conk him over the head with a lead pipe – then chop him up and put him in the freezer, then put the frozen parts into one of those tree shreddin' machines like that man did up in...in...in...Minnesota! Or one of them north cold states to his wife. It was on "60 Minutes."...or Rolanda or RuPaul...

**WILLI.** *(wistfully)* Oh, RuPaul.

**LA SONIA.** Anyway, when the snow melted they found little bitty pieces, like hair and shit – DNA, just like in the O.J. trial — and they tested it and they determined it was her. The wife. Gonna fry his ass too. He on death row now. His mistake was he shoulda backed that tree shreddin' machine up to a lake, then his wife's pieces woulda got eaten up by the little fishes and he woulda walked away scott free. But the dumb shit didn't think it through. Stopped too early. You gotsta think these things through, Willi baby.

**WILLI.** *(thinks)* So where do you suppose I can get a tree shreddin' machine?

*(They howl.)*

**LA SONIA.** That's my girl. We put our minds to it, I bet we could find us one. Grab them want ads, girl.

**WILLI.** We're goin' to hell.

**LA SONIA.** Hell yeah, we goin' to hell!

*(They laugh harder.)*

I sure bet we could find us a tree shreddin' machine. Then we could pulverize ol' J.D. and make fish food outta him. *(looks at watch)* Ooh, I gotta go. LaVell done faked sick and come home early to love on me. That man can never gets enough lovin' – and I'm here to tell you, I got enough about ten, twelve years ago.

**WILLI.** Now you're the one who's a liar. You're just sayin' that to show out.

**LA SONIA.** *(smiles, yes she is)* I am not. It makes me tired and I'm already tired because of loud neighbors fightin', keeping me awake at night.

*(They hug.)*

**WILLI.** I'll see you tomorrow.

**LA SONIA.** Yes ma'am, you will.

*(She starts to exit, then turns back, having unsnapped her blouse. Underneath is a low-cut teddy, showing off* **LA SONIA***'s big beautiful breasts.)*

Woo, hoo!

*(***WILLI** *turns, is stunned and laughs as* **LA SONIA** *struts.)*

**WILLI.** It all makes sense now. It all makes sense. *(Remembering, points to portable TV.)* TV.

*(***LA SONIA** *buttons up her blouse as she goes for the TV.)*

**LA SONIA.** Oh, I read in the Peoples Magazine that some woman kilt two of her husbands by givin' them some undetectable poison called ethylene glycol. I'll get on the internet and get us some of that.

*(There is a knock on the door.)*

**WILLI.** Well, who in the world?

*(***LA SONIA** *rushes to the door, beating* **WILLI** *to it.)*

**LA SONIA.** Oooh it's number seventeen.

(**WILLI** *looks over* **LA SONIA**'s *shoulder.* **RAYLEEN** *doesn't see them.*)

**WILLI.** With my empty Pyrex dish. Lord, she does not look good in the light of day, bless her heart. *(opening door)* Hello there, Rayleen. Come on in.

(**RAYLEEN** *enters carrying a Pyrex dish, puffing on a cigarette, wearing a halter top and cut-off jean shorts – and she does look less than stunning.* **WILLI** *can't stop staring at her.* **LA SONIA** *quickly moves behind the couch, evaluating* **RAYLEEN***, blocked from her view by* **WILLI***.*)

**RAYLEEN.** I just brung back your dish. That cherry delight was…dee-lightful. *(She laughs.)*

**WILLI.** Thank you. But it's cherry *dump* delight. It's my Aunt Glenda's recipe. It's my husband's favorite dessert. In fact, I'm gonna make one for him tonight.

**RAYLEEN.** Well, it was just dee-light-ful and dee-licious and I could just kill you! I could feel my ass growin' with every fuckin' bite.

**WILLI.** You could stand to put on a few if you ask me. You have a darlin' little figure.

(**WILLI** *opens the door window and waves away the smoke.* **RAYLEEN***, in consideration, crosses to the window and blows her smoke out.*)

**RAYLEEN.** Thank you. I guess I keep in good shape because I'm on my feet a lot.

**LA SONIA.** *(under her breath)* On her feet.

(**WILLI** *shoots* **LA SONIA** *a look.*)

**RAYLEEN.** You know with my job. Runnin' around, tryin' to please drunks. That's my entire workout routine. I keep my arms toned by smokin'. I switch arms with every other cigarette so one arm dudn't get bigger than the other. I figure if I'm gonna catch cancer from smokin', I oughta get some benefits out of it.

**WILLI.** *(laughs)* Oh, you are funny. I needed a good laugh.

(**LA SONIA** *clears her throat.*)

Oh, I'm sorry. This is my friend, LaSonia. I don't think y'all've met.

**RAYLEEN.** Hi. I've seen you around, La –

**LA SONIA.** Sonia.

**RAYLEEN.** I see. Interesting. Well, it's a pleasure to meet you.

(*She extends her hand.* **LA SONIA** *looks at her hand, but makes no effort to reciprocate.*)

**LA SONIA.** Um, hum. I see you're all dressed for a hot day. Or should I say undressed.

(**LA SONIA** *throws a look to* **WILLI.**)

**RAYLEEN.** (*laughs*) That's a good 'un. Undressed for a hot day. I'm gonna have to remember that one.

**LA SONIA.** It's all yours, sista. You'll probably get more use out of it than I will.

**RAYLEEN.** Well, yes. Fuck, yeah. This fuckin' heat is just fuckin' evil.

**WILLI.** Indeed it is.

(**LA SONIA** *goes and grabs the TV.*)

**LA SONIA.** Well, I better go tend to my wifely duties so I can get on the *fuckin'* internet and do our research… (*Whispers to* **WILLI** *as she passes her.*)…on how to kill your *fuckin'* husband. I'll be back in a little while.

(*She exits laughing.*)

**RAYLEEN.** (*calling out door*) Nice meetin' you, La…

**LA SONIA.** (*O.S.*) Sonia!

**WILLI.** LaSonia's husband LaVell faked sick and come home early to love on her. Idn't that sweet.

**RAYLEEN.** Precious.

**WILLI.** LaVell works on the loadin' dock over at the Super Wal-Mart. A real good place to work from what I understand. Lots of benefits. They have a real good marriage.

**RAYLEEN.** Wal-Mart has single handedly destroyed the small businessman in the South. Don't get me started on Wal-Mart. It's just too early. I refuse to shop at Wal-Mart unless it's real late at night and I need toilet paper or Tater Tots. I sometimes get a cravin' for Tater Tots after work. Other than that, I draw the line.

**WILLI.** Well, they do have good prices.

**RAYLEEN.** That does not impress me one iota. It's playin' footsies with the devil, but don't get me started on Wal-Mart. It's just too early.

**WILLI.** Okay.

**RAYLEEN.** Your friend's a real crack up. Their kind always have a good sense of humor. I used to work with this black gal named Chavante over in Mineola and she worked the back room where they all hung out. I mean they could sit up in the front bar when the laws changed back when and all, but they were just more comfortable in the back with their own kind and they'd just laugh and jaw back there. It'd leak out. I'm here to tell you, you put a bunch of 'em in a room together, throw in some cheap liquor, they can cut up! Listen at me already runnin' my mouth. "Diarrhea of the mouth." That's what my third husband Jimmy Ray used to say to me. He's in the pen for shooting a mean cop over in Waco, who was always harassing him for speeding.

**WILLI.** Lord!

**RAYLEEN.** Don't worry. The cop didn't die. He hit him in the saliva gland and his shoulder, basically just winged him. But he got caught and that was all she wrote. Thirty-five years, no possibility of parole, so the marriage was basically over. Hard to make that work. And don't get me started on them cogical *(pronounced ca-gi-cal)* visits. It's just too early. Them prison mattresses. No sheets. *(wistfully)* Jimmy Ray'll be seventy-two when he gets out. Hard to wait on that, know what I mean. Jimmy Ray was the only man I ever really loved, but he had anger issues.

**WILLI.** Sounds it.

**RAYLEEN.** I stopped visitin' him. It was just too hard on both of us. All that love, separated by a Plexiglas partition. Plus, the drive was just ungodly. I got three speeding tickets. I got stopped seven or eight times, but I flirted my way out of them other tickets. But not three of 'em. Those cops were unbending. Probably gay. I read somewhere there's a lot of gay cops. Makes sense to me.

**WILLI.** I guess.

*(Long awkward pause. **RAYLEEN** tosses her cigarette out the door, then just stands there.)*

*(finally)* Well, come on in and set a spell.

**RAYLEEN.** Okay.

*(She ushers **RAYLEEN** to the couch.)*

**WILLI.** Since it's kinda like mornin' to you, would you like some coffee? Still some in the Mr. Coffee there.

**RAYLEEN.** I'd love some. Strong and black. Just like my men. *(laughs)* I's just kiddin'. That's the farthest thing from the truth. They've all been weak and white. My men. *(distant)* My strang of men.

**WILLI.** Well, I've been married since I was seventeen. J.D. and me were high school sweethearts. Back then, he was the quarterback and ever' girl in our school wanted that sexy boy that rode the motorcycle. I was the envy of them all back then.

*(hands **RAYLEEN** her coffee)*

Here ya go.

**RAYLEEN.** Thanks. *(re: Want Ads)* You lookin' for a job? Ooh, this coffee is good and strong, just like I like it.

**WILLI.** Oh, let me get those out of your way. *(taking them)* No, I was just doodling. Pretending.

*(**WILLI** throws away the paper. Awkward pause.)*

My son is gay. He's not a cop. He lives in St. Louis these days. My husband won't talk to him or about him and forbids me to as well. Kicked him out when he was sixteen when he found him with the preacher's boy doin'…well, thangs.

**RAYLEEN.** Thangs?

**WILLI.** But sometimes I save my change and sneak over to the pay phone outside the Wash 'N Fold. I mostly just get his machine, but it's always good to hear his voice. He was my single purpose in life. Well, him and his sister. I don't know how LaSonia does it. She's barren and since she lost her job when the Catfish Hut went belly up, she's just obsessed with the internet.

**RAYLEEN.** I don't get the internet. And I can't wrap my mind around fish tacos either. Fish does not belong in a taco shell. Don't get me started on that. It's just too early.

**WILLI.** I won't. His name is John David. My son. He's a junior. John David Winkler, Jr. Was always such a sweet, sensitive boy. I had a daughter too – Melissa – but she was killed in a real bad car wreck when she was sixteen. I lost both of my children when they were sixteen. J.D. said I spoiled them both rotten, turned my son gay and caused my daughter to be rebellious and was overprotective. She was runnin' with the wrong crowd when she was killed. J.D. won't even let me keep pictures of them in the house, but I keep a couple hidden. Lord, now it's me that's runnin' at the mouth. I shouldn'ta told you all that.

**RAYLEEN.** Well, I'm such an open book I tend to get people to just spill the beans real fast like. Story of my life.

**WILLI.** *(distant)* Funny. I don't think I was protective enough.

*(**RAYLEEN** gets up, walks around, exploring pictures and knick-knacks during:)*

**RAYLEEN.** I'm sorry about your daughter. And the circumstances of your son. I never lost a child, never had one. I did have a Pekingese dog once named Lil' Bit that my second husband Pup runned over while Lil' Bit was doin' his business. Always did his business in the driveway. Preferred the gravel, don't ask me why. Squashed Lil' Bit flatter than a pancake. It's more than a little odd that a person named Pup killed my Pekingese dog, don't you think?

**WILLI.** That's what you call ironic.

**RAYLEEN.** Ironic. That's not his real name of course. Pup. Nickname. For the life of me I can't remember his real name. I can't imagine losing a child, Willi. That musta been awful.

**WILLI.** I almost fell apart, but life goes on.

**RAYLEEN.** *(distant)* And on and on and on and on.

**WILLI.** Listen, don't tell J.D. I told you about John David or my daughter. And don't tell him you visited me or that LaSonia was here. He has quirks about all that. If it were up to J.D., I'd just sit here all by my lonesome, day end, day out.

**RAYLEEN.** Tic-a-lock, tic-a-lock. I won't say a word. Being gay is just a mystery to me. Lesbianism even more so.

**WILLI.** Well, I always say we only understand us and then it gets real fuzzy.

**RAYLEEN.** I agree. Whew. That is profound. I need to write that 'un down. You are smart as a whip, Willi.

**WILLI.** *(modest)* Well –

*(**RAYLEEN** settles at the kitchen table. **WILLI** takes the cling peaches out of the refrigerator and gives a bowl to **RAYLEEN**, takes one for herself, then settles at the table with **RAYLEEN**, intently listening.)*

**RAYLEEN.** I onced had this job at this nasty little roadside bar called The Dew Drop Inn. Real original, huh? Right outside of Ponder, Texas. Bumfuck! The owner was this big-boned gal named Mona Burke and I always suspected, you know. She'd flirt with me like a man would, always with a big ol' smile in that deep voice say – *(deep voice)* "Hey Leena…" That's what she called me. Leena.

**WILLI.** Leena. That's cute.

**RAYLEEN.** I don't really like it, please don't call me that. But I was kinda scared of her, so I didn't say anything.

**WILLI.** I'll just call you Rayleen.

**RAYLEEN.** That'll work. Anyway, Mona'd say – *(deep voice)* "Hey Leena, I sure do like that skirt your a wearin'" or "Hey Leena, that blouse sure does ac-cen-tu-ate your tits." She'd say that when I was showin' 'em off, which was pretty much all the time because – more tits, more tips – a little trick to the trade. Well, one night me and Mona started drankin' after work and we somehow, all the specifics have just gone out the winda, but we somehow winded up back at her trailer that sat out behind the Dew Drop. And that night, well, thangs happened.

**WILLI.** Things happened?

**RAYLEEN.** Uh-huh. Little bit. They did. Lord! I should just shut my fuckin' trap right here and now 'cause I *should* not be tellin' you this.

**WILLI.** *(quickly)* You can't stop now. I mean, I'm enjoying your story.

**RAYLEEN.** Okay. Well, let's see, where was I?

**WILLI.** Where thangs happened.

**RAYLEEN.** It all started with a crick in my neck. So I kept rubbin' my neck and ol' Mona took note, you know, and she moved in over by me on the love seat and started givin' me a massage, neck rub, and her rubbin' my shoulders felt so good, you know – I was in between husbands and it had been a long time since I had been touched by anybody – and before you know it, I don't know how, but Mona winded up between my legs…

**WILLI.** Oh my stars…

**RAYLEEN.** …my panties around my ankles, skirt hiked up to Jesus and she commenced to lap like a thirsty yard dog on a hot Texas day.

**WILLI.** Sweet baby Jesus.

**RAYLEEN.** And let me tell you something, Willi, that ol' big-boned gal knew exactly what she was a doin'. She knew where ever'thang was. She knew how to please.

**WILLI.** Lordy, lordy.

**RAYLEEN.** You want me to stop, is this gettin' too graphic, 'cause I could stop if I'm offendin'.

**WILLI.** No, no! I watch Maury Povich *and* Jerry Springer.

**RAYLEEN.** Well, she was goin' at it full force. And I started shudderin' and writhin' about on that love seat. I was so wet that love seat just turned into one of them Slip And Slides. It was covered in plastic, which I don't get. I mean you buy a new couch and keep the plastic on. Not right. So we was slippin' and slidin' and girl, I was about to come unglued. Hell, I bet I came at least six times straight, I mean, I was ready to go through the roof. Ready to explode. Then all of a sudden, ol' Mona popped out and said, "Hey Leena, turn about's fair play."

**WILLI.** Uh-oh.

**RAYLEEN.** Exactly! Well, that's when reality smacked me hard, I mean *hard*, Willi. All of sudden, I was sober as a judge and I gulped and musta looked like I was about to shit myself, I guess, 'cause Mona Burke just busted out laughin' and blurted out, "Hey, Leena, you *are* straight! You're just drunk!" And we commenced to talk and jaw and drank until sun up and I gained so much respect for Mona that night. "Turn about's fair play." Shit. Fuck. Hell. Damnation. "Turn about's fair play." Can you imagine?

**WILLI.** No, I cannot.

**RAYLEEN.** I shouldn'ta told you all that. You'll never respect me now.

**WILLI.** Oh, honey, that story doesn't change the way I feel about you.

**RAYLEEN.** You know, I don't think I've never heard of anyone called "Lasagna."

**WILLI.** Her name is really LaSonia. She pronounces it "Lasagna" like the noodle dish, but it's spelled L-A-S-O-N-I-A. The "S" is capital. Most folks would just say LaSonia. But you know how creative they are with names.

**RAYLEEN.** I do, I do.

**WILLI.** LaSonia is my very best friend in the whole wide world. She's the best person I know.

**RAYLEEN.** Well, I'll tell you one thing for dang sure. I would not want to be named after a fuckin' noodle dish.

**WILLI.** You know, I'm not being judgmental, but I don't believe I've ever heard a woman use that word so much. You know the "F" word. Sometimes I think it and wish I could use it, but I just don't have the nerve.

**RAYLEEN.** Oh, don't start, Willi. It's a terrible habit. I picked it up from my second husband Pup. For the life of me I can't remember his real name. Pup said "fuck" all the time, so I just picked it up – plus, it has to do with working in bars and dating worthless men. Of course, those days are over. I'm single for life now.

**WILLI.** You swore off marriages?

**RAYLEEN.** I had to. I've been married five times. It's against the law to marry more than five times in the state of Texas. My sister Lucinda, the Bible thumper, told me that.

**WILLI.** I've never heard about that five-times marriage law. I thought Sue Nell Parker who used to live in space number eleven had been married seven times, but I could be mistaken.

**RAYLEEN.** Your friend probably married some of her husbands out of state. Vegas will tolerate as many marriages as you want. All about capitalism, don't get me started. Frankly, I don't have the time or the energy to get married again. Parnell! That was Pup's real name. Parnell Jenkins. Mean as a snake. Lord, look at the time. I better get a move on. I've got to reapply and get to work.

**WILLI.** You certainly have lived a colorful life. Please stop by any time, just don't tell J.D.

**RAYLEEN.** Well, I'll temper my visits. I've been known to wear out a welcome. I would invite you over, but my place is so teeny that the only way two people can fit is if they're horizontal. *(laughs)*

**WILLI.** You are such a liberal, Rayleen.

**RAYLEEN.** I'll see you later, Willi.

*(***RAYLEEN*** *exits.)*

**WILLI.** Bye bye. Lord have pity on my soul. *(She has a panic attack, deep breaths.)* I'm not gonna shrivel up and die. I'm not gonna shrivel up and die. I'm not gonna shrivel up and die. *(better, then looks at the clock)* Oh, Lord, J.D.

*(Lights up in the bar and ***J.D.*** enters.)*

**J.D.** Hey, Rayleen.

*(No answer. He sits at his table.)*

*(In the trailer, ***WILLI*** puts the steak in the skillet, turns the stove on, sets the table, checks the time. A truck drives by. She runs to the door, opens it, watches as it passes by. She closes the door, sighs. The ***PIANIST*** enters and begins to play as the ***BLUES SINGER*** appears in the wings. ***WILLI*** sits at the kitchen table and stares out the*

*"window" accomplished by lighting cue as the* **BLUES SINGER** *sings "The Waiting Game."*)

**BLUES SINGER.**

Sittin' starin' out the window
Lookin' at a cold gray sky.
And there you wait.
You wait and you wonder,
"Lord, how much longer
Will life keep passin' me by?"

(**RAYLEEN** *rushes into the bar, now dressed for work.* **J.D.** *slaps her on the ass. She gives him a dirty look, then goes over, puts her purse behind the bar, delivers a beer to* **J.D.**, *glares at him. She goes back, wipes down the bar, then walks to the edge of the bar and stares out, matching* **WILLI***'s stares – strong mirrored staging throughout the song with* **WILLI** *and* **RAYLEEN** *heighten the power of the scene.*)

Yeah, you're waitin' for the sunshine.
You'd even settle for some rain.
Just need a change.
Need somethin' to hope for.
Worse than not livin'
Is livin' but feelin' no pain.

(*She is now singing to both* **WILLI** *and* **RAYLEEN**. **WILLI** *gets up and goes to the recipe box, pulls out the pictures.* **J.D.** *goes and spins* **RAYLEEN** *around. Simultaneously,* **WILLI** *spins and begins "dancing" with the pictures of her children, while* **J.D.** *begins to dance with an initially reluctant* **RAYLEEN**.)

Waiting to leave the past.
Waiting for something real.
Waiting for good to last.
Waiting for wounds to heal.
It can drive you insane…
Playing this Waiting Game.

(**WILLI** *goes to the couch as* **J.D.** *takes* **RAYLEEN***'s hands*

*and leads her out of the bar, simultaneous movement.*
**RAYLEEN** *pauses for a moment, looks back, seemingly right at* **WILLI**. *But she's weak and exits with* **J.D.** *as the* **BLUES SINGER** *moves into the bar, settling by the piano now singing right to* **WILLI**.)

**BLUES SINGER.**

Always waitin' for the laughter.

Waitin' for your ship to come in.

Those simple dreams

That everyone clings to

Like waiting for love.

Waiting for life to begin.

*(**WILLI** sits on the couch, staring at the pictures, then she begins to cry, this time letting it all out as the **BLUES SINGER** tries to penetrate the walls, the pain, the damage with her message.)*

Waiting for anything.

If just to smile again.

A different song to sing.

A life that might have been.

*(Lights fade, leaving only a soft spot on the **BLUES SINGER**.)*

It's a crying shame,

Playing the Waiting Game.

Lord, it's always the same…

Playing this Waiting Game.

*(Lights out in the bar, then low lights inch up in the trailer. **WILLI** sleeps on the couch. It's quiet. Eerie quiet. A truck starts. **WILLI** wakes up, then gets up and looks out the door. Her face drops. She watches for a long time, then frantically hides the pictures back in the recipe box, covers her mouth, then hits her head with her palm over and over as **J.D.**'s truck circles the trailer court, then pulls up in their driveway. She stands there, back to the door, as the familiar steps on gravel come towards the trailer. **J.D.** enters, sets lunchbox in sink.)*

**J.D.** I had to go down to Waco and my truck overheated and there was no way to call.

**WILLI.** It's eleven-thirty at night.

**J.D.** Yeah, it is. You can read time.

**WILLI.** I made you pan-fried steak and cherry dump delight –

**J.D.** I done ate. Stick it in the frigerdare. I'll eat 'em tomorrow. I'm tired.

**WILLI.** Okay.

*(He exits down the hallway.* **WILLI** *stands there, starts to put away the food. Her hands begin to shake, she drops a bowl, then calls out).*

I saw you come out of her camper shell.

**J.D.** *(O.S.)* What?

**WILLI.** I saw you come out of number seventeen's camper shell –

*(***J.D.*** appears at the door and starts towards her, her back to him.)*

– and knock over one of them gnomes and go down the road and get your pickup from behind the bend, then drive up. *(losing it, wheels on him)* I saw you! I know what you did! I saw you, J.D. and I was sitting here waiting all night long after'n I had made your favorite supper, scrapin' ever' cent I could find for your stupid steak while you was doin' what you was doin' with her –

**J.D.** *(pause, menacing)* You. Didn't. See. Shit. I had truck trouble down right outside of Mexia. *(pronounced Mahey-uh)* So you must of dozed off and had a dream or was hallucinating or else you have lost your mind and have gone off your rocker. Now I'm going to bed now because I've been working hard all day and am dog tared and I better *never* ever hear another word about this *if* you know what's good for you.

*(***WILLI*** looks down.)*

You understand? You understand, woman? *(Knocks lunch box into sink.)* Look at me when I'm talkin' to you!!

*(***WILLI*** looks up quickly.)*

You. Didn't. See. Shit.

*(He gives* **WILLI** *a shove, then another, then turns and walks down the hall, muttering:)*

You talk that shit to J.D. Winkler, that's the last thing you'll do.

*(***WILLI*** *stares after him as he exits, a volcano about to erupt. She rushes to the hallway door.)*

**WILLI.** *(screaming)* I saw you! I saw you!!!

*(***J.D.*** *flies to the door, grabs her hair and pulls her into the hallway and begins beating her in front of the window. The shadows of punching and the beating as* **WILLI** *screams. Silence. The* **PIANIST** *begins to play as* **WILLI** *returns to the doorway, holding her arm, crying. Soft spot comes up on the* **BLUES SINGER**, *one more time trying to reach* **WILLI** *with her reprise of "The Waiting Game.")*

**BLUES SINGER.**

What are you waiting for?

Don't let another day go by.

Can't wait anymore.

It's time you learn how to fly.

Cryin's over,

You're not to blame

For playing the Waiting Game.

So tired of this Waiting Game.

No…

No more of this Waiting Game.

*(***WILLI*** *wipes her eyes, makes a decision, walks over and grabs the cherry dump delight out of the stove and throws it in the trash. She starts to walk away, then returns to the trash, digs out the want ads, reads them for a moment, then looks up with hope.)*

*(BLACKOUT)*

### End of Act Two

# ACT THREE

*(In darkness, we hear a rousing piano intro. Lights come up on the* **BLUES SINGER**, *wearing a red church dress, and she performs "If You Believe, You Can Achieve.")*

**BLUES SINGER.**

Ol' Moses was told to deliver

His people from bondage and pain.

And Moses scratched his head and said,

"My God, are you insane?

Where shall we go?

How can we leave?"

And the Lord said, "Mo,

Brother, don't you know

If You Believe, You Can Achieve."

*(***WILLI** *scurries out from the hallway. Her hair is coifed and she wears a long sleeve light peach cotton blouse and a khaki skirt, dressed for an interview.)*

If You Believe, You Can Achieve.

If You Believe, You Can Achieve.

Even in your darkest hour,

Keep the faith.

You have the power!

Anything is possible

If You Believe.

*(The* **BLUES SINGER** *crosses into the trailer, goes to* **WILLI**, *hands her her purse, touches her hurt arm, seemingly heals it, then gently pushes her towards the door.* **WILLI** *exits.)*

**BLUES SINGER.**

> So Moses, he gathered his people
> And they marched to that sea so red.
> With no way to cross,
> With no boat to float,
> They cried, "We're sunk!
> We're dead!"
>
> Moses, he prayed.
> Prayed with all his heart.
>
> And the Lord, He smiled.
> "Just believe, my child."
> And don't you know,
> That sea sho nuff did part.
>
> *(The* **BLUES SINGER** *motions and* **WILLI** *enters what was the bar area. The* **BLUES SINGER** *grabs a [preset] Wal-Mart vest and a Wal-Mart name tag that reads "Willadean" and puts it on* **WILLI** *during:)*
>
> If You Believe, You Can Achieve.
> Yes, If You Believe, You Can Achieve.
> Even in your darkest hour,
> Keep the faith.
> You have the power!
> Anything is possible
> If You Believe.
>
> *(The* **BLUES SINGER** *pushes* **WILLI** *into a pool of light.)*

**WILLI.** Welcome to Wal-Mart. How may I help you? Is that a return? Let me put a little pink sticker on that for you. Oh, isn't that the most precious child God ever made? Here's you a little smiley face sticker.

**BLUES SINGER.**

> If You Believe, You Can Achieve.
> Yes, If You Believe, You Can Achieve.
> Just like them in the Bible story,
> You can follow that Road to Glory!

Anything is possible
If You Believe.

Oh, just believe with all your heart and soul.
And know
That you can find a purpose to put in motion.
Move a mountain
Or swim an ocean.
It's a powerful thing,
Devotion.
Ask, ye shall receive!
If You Believe, You Can Achieve.
Lord, If You Believe, You Can Achieve.

If the worst should happen to ya,
Don't give up,
Just say "Hallelujah!"
You can do what you set your mind to.
Learn to free all the ties that bind you.
Anything is possible if you believe.

*(She steps right up to* **WILLI**, *strokes her face,* **WILLI** *stares right at her.)*

I say,
Every little thing is possible
If you…
Lord, if you…

*(***WILLI*** *reaches out and puts a yellow smiley sticker on the* **BLUES SINGER**'s *dress.)*

**WILLI.** Thank you for shoppin' at Wal-Mart!

**BLUES SINGER.**

*(wailing)* Just believe!!!!

*(BLACKOUT)*

*(Music transition.* **BLUES SINGER** *exits and lights inch up in the trailer as* **WILLI** *approaches her trailer. She bangs on* **LA SONIA**'s *trailer.)*

**WILLI.** *(calling)* LaSonia! LaSonia! I'm home.

**LA SONIA.** *(O.S.)* I'll be right there. I'm just signin' off.

> **(WILLI** *enters her trailer, closes the door, then looks out the door window towards* **RAYLEEN**'s *trailer.)*

**WILLI.** There you are. Over there sleepin'. How you can sleep at night – or in the middle of the day – I'll never know. Eatin' my cherry dump delight, then doin' no tellin' what you done with my husband. I bet turn about was fair play with him all right. Well…*(She raises the window and spews:)* Fuck you! You fuckin' bitch.! *(Slams the window shut.)* There! I did it! I finally used the "F" word. Twice. One for both of 'em.

**LA SONIA.** *(O.S.)* Willi! I'm comin'. *(enters)* Where you been all morning? We done missed "Maury," "Texas Justice," "Oprah" and "Judge Judy"!

**WILLI.** I got a job, LaSonia! Look! I got myself a job. They hired me on the spot at the Super Wal-Mart. I'm a Wal-Mart greeter!

**LA SONIA.** *(with disdain)* A greeter?

**WILLI.** I applied first thing this morning and they put me right to work. Said I was just what they were lookin' for – Wal-Mart material!

*(She puts on her vest, models it.)*

**LA SONIA.** *(This is not good.)* Oh, Willi baby.

**WILLI.** Look, I got my own name tag. I decided to go with Willadean. Everybody's always just called me plain ol' Willi but now…well, now, I'm somebody. I'm a Wal-Mart greeter and I have a name tag with my given name. Willadean. *(assumes work pose)* Welcome to Wal-mart. How may I help you?

*(**LA SONIA** just stares at her.)*

I'm not going to tell him. I have a plan and you're in on it.

**LA SONIA.** You have a plan and I'm in on it?

**WILLI.** Yes, ma'am. See, you're gonna keep my uniform and name tag over at your house and I'll get it right before I go to work and –

**LA SONIA.** Willi, you can't pull this off.

**WILLI.** What you believe you can achieve, LaSonia. I got the job, now I'm going to figure out a way to keep it without him ever even knowing. It's like God worked it out. I work from eight in the morning 'til noon. Five days a week. No weekends. Told them it was against my religion. J.D. leaves for work at five-thirty, so I'm all clear. He's on short haul routes these days and will be out of this town every day until late afternoon when he stops by The Spotlight for his beers, then comes home for his supper – so I'll be home with food on the table and what he don't know won't hurt him.

**LA SONIA.** But if he do know, he'll hurt you and you know it. What if he gets sick? Stays home? You can't do this, baby. He gonna find out.

**WILLI.** No, he won't! If he stays home, then I'll call in sick. I have sick days too. And personal days. I'll walk down to the Wash 'N Fold and call in sick. What you believe you can achieve, LaSonia! They are paying me five dollars and forty cents an hour! I'm going to make one hundred and eight dollars a week. And get this. Mrs. Font, the personnel woman at the Super Wal-Mart, told me that if I'm a good employee, that I can transfer to another store in six months.

**LA SONIA.** Girl, what you talkin' about? Only one Super Wal-Mart here in Mesquite.

**WILLI.** I'm going to leave him, LaSonia. Save my money, get my transfer and leave. I'm going to move up to St. Louis and be near my boy. I miss John David so much, LaSonia. I need to ask for forgiveness. Else I'm gonna shrivel up and die.

**LA SONIA.** Then I guess you don't need this.

*(She produces printed-out papers, hands them to* **WILLI.***)*

**WILLI.** What's this?

**LA SONIA.** Ways to kill your husband and not get caught. I did my research on the internet just like I promised.

*(***WILLI*** sits on the couch, studying the research.)*

**WILLI.** You did all this research on how I can kill my husband and not get caught? You are so sweet. Thank you for being such a good friend. *(looking at list)* Lord! Shooting a shringe full of air in his veins?

**LA SONIA.** That's the best way in my opinion. Called "Death by Air Injection" and all you need is a shringe full of air. They sell 'em at Wal-Mart for diabetics. *(realizing)* Oh! You get an employee discount now! The trick is hittin' a vein, Willi, but if he passed out drunk, you can do it. What you believe, you can achieve!

**WILLI.** LaSonia, I think I'm just gonna stick with my plan of workin' at Wal-Mart and movin' to St. Louis. All this worries me about you.

**LA SONIA.** I gots me a criminal mind all right. LaVell always tellin' me that. But you know I never acts on it.

**WILLI.** Well, you take this nonsense with you. I am not about to kill J.D. Although after what he did with number seventeen, I certainly understand why women do it. And that's why I got my job. I'm not doin' nothin' else he tells me to do – or not to do. He was cheatin' on me, LaSonia.

**LA SONIA.** I know, baby girl.

**WILLI.** You knew and you didn't tell me?

**LA SONIA.** Because there would have been a fight – just like there was when you *did* find out – and he would have beat you up again! That's why. I saw him come out of her trailer that night he beat you up over the TV breakin'.

**WILLI.** *(realizing)* He made love to me that night.

**LA SONIA.** I was just hopin' you would never find out, but you did and – All night long I heard the two of you fightin', goin' at it. Where'd he get you this time?

*(LA SONIA starts her inspection routine.)*

**WILLI.** LaSonia, I've had a real good day and I don't need any of your questions. Not today.

**LA SONIA.** I want to tell you what happened to my sister –

**WILLI.** I don't want to know what happened, LaSonia! Can't you get it through your head that I don't want to know!

**LA SONIA.** Well, tough shit! It's time you need to listen to me because you went and got yourself a job at the Super Wal-Mart and this is a small town and J.D. will find out and he will beat the livin' shit out of you for that and for the next thing and for the next and one day he will kill you if you don't do somethin' like shoot his vein with a shringe full of air. And if you don't do somethin', it's gonna be too late and you may not make it six months to get your transfer to St. Louis and see your boy and ask him to forgive you! So you sit your lily white ass down, Wil-la-dean Winkler, *right now* – and listen to this story about my baby sister! Today!!!

**WILLI.** Okay.

*(**WILLI** sits on the sofa, **LA SONIA** sits next to her.)*

**LA SONIA.** *(takes her time, calmly)* She was wearin' this hat. A bright red hat. And it was Easter Sunday morning at the Ebanezar Baptist Church. Child, it was a sea of hats. The sistas can wear themselves some hats on Easter Sunday morning. But my baby sister had on the prettiest hat of all – or maybe it was that that hat framed her beautiful face and it just seemed that her red hat was the prettiest. Or maybe I was just partial. We sat together and sang "He Arose" and "At the Cross" and my baby sister's favorite "Victory in Jesus." *(singing)* "Oh victory in Jesus, my savior for…" Yes ma'am, we sang to the top of our lungs and we felt happy. My people can sing, Willi baby, they sure 'nough can sing. But after we sang, in the middle of the sermon, I looked down – and peaking out from under her long-sleeve red Easter dress – she always wore red dresses – I saw the bruises. And I reached down and ever so gently lifted the sleeve and there were the bruises. The bruises were everywhere. I knew. I knew exactly what was happening and I vowed to Jesus that Easter Sunday morning in a pew at the Ebanezar Baptist Church that I was going to go over the next morning and we were going to pack her up and she was going to leave that poor excuse for a man. And I did. I gave her the LaSonia "what for" speech and my beautiful baby sister listened to me and we did it. Packed up all her things and we had ourselves a plan. See, we knew if we just left, he'd come find her. Bring her back. She had done tried that before. But, if she told him she was leavin' with all her stuff packed up sittin' there, we knew he'd go crazy, start in on her – and that was part of our plan. But timin' was crucial. When she heard him drive up, she was s'pose to call the police, then hang up and call me. The police would show up in the middle of the storm, arrest that bastard, then I would swoop on in for the rescue. It was a good plan, Willi baby. But…*(chokes up)*…she never did call the cops – or me. I don't know what happened. Maybe she didn't hear him drive up. I don't know. I don't know what happened. When they called me to identify her body, her beautiful face was so bashed in we couldn't even give her a proper viewing. We sang her favorite song, "Victory In Jesus" at her funeral – but there was no victory in nobody, Willi. Just defeat. I lost my baby sister, Willi. That's the last time I went to church because I thought – If God allowed this to happen – if this was "His will" like Brother Johnson preached at my sister's funeral, then I didn't want no part – *(She can't continue. Tears tumble down both faces.)* And I heard y'all fighin' last night. Then silence. Just silence. And I sat over there scared outta my ever' lovin' mind wantin' to come and check on you, but scared to interfere because last time I interfered –

*(**WILLI** gets up to get a box of tissues, gives one to **LA SONIA**, comforts her for a moment.)*

Now you know why I needed to tell you about my sister.

**WILLI.** I'm sorry. I'm so sorry.

**RAYLEEN.** *(O.S.)* Willi!!!

**LA SONIA.** Oh, shit.

**RAYLEEN.** *(O.S.)* Willi!!!

*(WILLI gets up and crosses to the door, looks out.)*

**WILLI.** Oooh, Lord, she's headin' over here.

**RAYLEEN.** *(calling O.S.)* Willi! Willi!!!! I need to talk to you.

**LA SONIA.** Hide!

*(LA SONIA exits down the hall. There is a knock. Louder. Now pounding.)*

**RAYLEEN.** Willi – *(pause)* Willi, I know you are in there with your friend. I'm all hitched up and heading out and I really want to talk to you in person before I scatter off into the wild blue yonder. Please can I come in just for a minute? Willi, please.

*(Will goes and opens the door.)*

Willi –

**WILLI.** Rayleen.

**RAYLEEN.** *(bursts into tears)* Oh Willi, I am so sorry I fucked your husband.

*(They stand there, **RAYLEEN** pleading with her eyes. **WILLI** stands, arms crossed.)*

**WILLI.** Well, we all make mistakes. *(pause)* Are you gonna be all right? You have money and all to get by?

**RAYLEEN.** Oh, fuck yeah. *(spots LA SONIA)* Hi. I got enough saved up to live for a stretch.

*(**LA SONIA** enters, stands in the doorway, arms crossed, glaring at **RAYLEEN**, exchanging looks with **WILLI**)*

**RAYLEEN.** And you know in my profession – cocktailin' – I have job security world wide. I've got my life all worked out these days – got a little home on wheels and within a hour or two, I can gather up my gnome collection, hitch my camper to my old trusty El Camino, then hit the road, on to the next place.

*(**RAYLEEN** plants herself on the couch, **LA SONIA** throws her arms up for **WILLI** – "can you believe her?")*

I see somewhere that looks nice or just have a feeling about a place, you know, find a trailer park, then scout out a nearby bar and bam! Back in business. But I always fuck it all up. Ever' decision I've ever made in my life has been wrong. *(chokes up)* Fuck. I really liked it here. But I can't stay, not after what I done to you. Oh, Willi, I am so sorry I fucked your husband.

*( LA SONIA grabs the cookie jar – gives WILLI a "this is going to be awhile" look – and goes and sits at the table.)*

**RAYLEEN.** It was a big lesson for me. You know not to fuck friend's husbands. It's a lot easier when you don't know the wives. I guess I always go for married men 'cause I can't get married again because of that five times married law, so if they're attached, I know I can't fall in love.

**LA SONIA.** That ain't true. Willi told me what your sister told you. I looked that up on the internet. She was lyin'.

**RAYLEEN.** What?!

**LA SONIA.** She lied to you. Ain't no such law in the state of Texas.

**RAYLEEN.** There's not?

**LA SONIA.** Uh, un.

**RAYLEEN.** We'll fuck me runnin'.

**LA SONIA.** I'm sure someone has.

**RAYLEEN.** Why that little bitch…you mean…fuck. Shit. Hell. I oughta drive over to Marfa right now and wring her neck.

**WILLI.** Well, you're already packed. *(pause)* Maybe now you can date someone single, have faith in love again. Find a good man, the marrying kind and clean up your life.

**LA SONIA.** *(in agreement)* Um-hum!

**RAYLEEN.** Yeah, that's a good idea. Your smart as a whip, Willi. *(pause, gets up, heads for door)* Shit, who the fuck am I foolin'? Who'd want a five times married cocktail waitress failure?

*(**RAYLEEN** stands by the door, awkward silent moment.)*

**WILLI.** Well, good luck, Rayleen.

*(**WILLI** pulls out a smiley sticker and places it on **RAYLEEN**'s tube top.)*

Keep smilin', Rayleen.

**RAYLEEN.** *(with every ounce of sincerity)* Willi, I am so sorry I fucked your husband.

*(***WILLI*** goes and hugs her,* ***RAYLEEN*** *crying.)*

It was nice meeting you, La…

**LA SONIA.** Sonia!

*(All of a sudden, a pickup truck squeals up.* ***WILLI*** *knows that sound and panics.)*

**WILLI.** It can't be. It's too early. *(looks out door, then turns back)* Oh, my God. It's J.D.!

**LA SONIA.** Shit!

**RAYLEEN.** *(overlap)* Shit!

**WILLI.** What's he doin' home this early?

*(***WILLI*** *rushes out to ward him off.)*

*(O.S.)* J.D. –

*(***J.D.*** *enters, pushing* ***WILLI*** *back in the house.)*

**J.D.** Get back in the house. Get in the goddamn house. NOW!

*(He stares at her uniform, then sees* ***RAYLEEN*** *and*

***LA SONIA****, then circles the couch.)*

Well, well, well. What do we have here? Welcome to the hen house. Bawk, bawk, bawk, cackle, cackle, cackle.

**WILLI.** J.D., what are you doin' – ?

**J.D.** *(overlap)* Shut up! *(to* ***RAYLEEN****)* I see you're leavin' town? *(walks over behind* ***LA SONIA****, looks down)* Nigger, get out of my house!

**LA SONIA.** You don't scare me, bully man. You don't scare me at –

*(***J.D.*** *suddenly pulls a gun out of his pants [hidden by shirt] and points the gun at the top of* ***LA SONIA****'s head. They all are terrified;* ***RAYLEEN*** *screams. NOTE: Read "additional Notes #3" in Props plot.)*

**J.D.** How 'bout now? Do I scare your big black ass now? Huh? Well, do I?

**WILLI.** *(overlap)* J.D., please!

**J.D.** Shut that flappin' trap of yours because I've got plenty to deal with you about! *(quiet and menacing to* ***LA SONIA****)* How'd ya like it if I put a bullet right through that nappy head of yours? Huh? And I'd get away with it too 'cause you are *trespassing on my property!!*

**WILLI.** J.D. –

**J.D.** *Shut up! Shut the fuck up!*

*(back to* **LA SONIA***, walking her out with gun to head)*

Now get out of my house and don't ever come back or I will kill you dead.

*(***LA SONIA*** rushes out.* **J.D.** *chases after her, waving the gun, during:)*

You worthless piece of trash! Well, go on if you want to live! *(yelling after her, standing outside door)* And don't even think about callin' the law because if I so much as hear, see or smell a cop, I will shoot Willi, then come back and riddle you with bullets. Fuckin' porch monkey.

*(***J.D.*** reenters;* **WILLI** *and* **RAYLEEN** *just stare in fear.)*

*(to* **RAYLEEN***)* What the fuck are you lookin' at, whore?! Huh?

**RAYLEEN.** I'm lookin' at trash, that's exactly what I'm lookin' at. Mean white trailer trash.

**J.D.** Hey pot! Kettle, you're black.

**RAYLEEN.** You ain't gonna get away with this.

*(Tears stream down* **WILLI***'s face as she watches.)*

**J.D.** Oh yes I am. YES I FUCKIN' AM!

*(She starts out, but* **J.D.** *blocks the door.)*

What'd she tell you, Willi? What'd this crazy bitch tell you?

**WILLI.** Nothin'. She didn't tell me nothin', J.D.

**J.D.** LIAR!!! You're a liar. What did this crazy fuckin' bitch tell you because…

*(suddenly grabbing* **RAYLEEN** *by the hair, pressing gun to her head.)*

…whatever she told you she's a goddamn liar. She come onto me and I turned her down and she threatened to tell you a pack of goddamn lies.

**RAYLEEN.** *(exploding)* You're the liar!!!

*(**RAYLEEN** smacks **J.D.**, pushes him.)*

Fuck! You are a crazy mother fucker. A certifiable crazy mother fucker. *(turns to **WILLI**)* I'm sorry, Willi. He's a damn liar and I'm a horrible horrible person....*(to **J.D.**)* But at least I know it!

**J.D.** Get the fuck out of my house!

*(He pushes and kicks at her as **RAYLEEN** rushes out, **J.D.** chasing after her.)*

*(calling after her)* You goddamn worthless two-bit beer joint waitress *whore* –!

*(He slams the door.)*

**WILLI.** J.D. –

**J.D.** *(low and menacing)* If you know what's good for you, you will be silent and let me do the talkin' 'til I'm done.

*(He goes over and slowly pulls down the blind in the door window, paces around **WILLI**, waving the gun, but not pointing it at her. He stalks around her, glaring, not saying anything for too long. He finally puts the gun on the bookshelf and grabs the Bible, holds it up.)*

"Wives, submit yourselves unto your husbands as unto the Lord." Ephesians 5:22. *(more stalking, pacing, glaring, getting louder)* "Wives, submit yourselves unto your husbands as unto the Lord. Wives, submit yourselves unto your own husbands as unto the Lord!" *(pacing, glaring)* So you got yourself a job, did ya?

**WILLI.** Yes. Yes, I did. I –

**J.D.** Take off that thing. That uniform thing. *Now.* Do it!

**WILLI.** No...no.

*(**J.D.** puts the Bible down, rushes **WILLI**, grabs her around the neck and forces the Wal-Mart smock off of her. He then takes the smock with her name tag, the dictionary and the Dr. Phil book and throws them in the oven, then goes and gets the kids' pictures out of the recipe box, throws them in the oven, too.)*

**J.D.** You didn't think I knew about these, did you? *(turns on oven)* I told you that no wife of mine is going to work. How do you think you made me look when Rooster's wife stopped by the hub to bring him his lunch and told me she saw you workin' at the Super Wal-Mart? Huh? And I could lose my job having to leave early to deal with your unsubmittin' ass, Willadean. Did you forget the Bible? Did you forget your upbringin'? *(He grabs the Bible again.)* They which commit such things are worthy of death!" Romans 1:32. *(He puts the Bible back on the bookshelf, pushing the gun behind it.)* That's God's Holy Word, Willadean, and you are worthy of death.

**WILLI.** What about you? You committed adultery. I know you did it, J.D. *(overlap, lines spewing, no pauses)*

**J.D.** No, I did not –

**WILLI.** Yes, you did. I know you did.

**J.D.** I did not!

**WILLI.** Yes, you –

**J.D.** All right, I fucked the bitch!! But you drove me to it. You drove me to everything. You drove me to this! YOU DROVE ME TO THIS!

**WILLI.** I'm keepin' my job –

**J.D.** YOU ARE NOT. No wife of mine is going to work.

**WILLI.** And I'm moving to St. Louis to be with my son and –

**J.D.** You are worthless.

**WILLI.** *(overlap)* I am not worthless –

**J.D.** You are a worthless piece of trailer trash –

**WILLI.** I am not worthless –

**J.D.** – and nobody will have you but me because you are worthless, Willadean. Worthless!!!!

**WILLI.** I AM NOT WORTHLESS. I AM NOT WORTH-LESS!!! AND YOU FUCKED HER, THEN YOU FUCKED ME!!!

*(**J.D.** rushes her – SLAP, SLAP, SLAP – then he pushes her, throws her behind the couch and starts beating and kicking her as she screams:)*

(*overlap during beating*) AHHHHHHHHHHHHHH-
HHH! NOOO! J.D. PLEASE! AHHHHH! J.D. PLEASE.
AHHHHHH!

(**J.D.** *continues to punch her, fist to face, fist to face.*)

**J.D.** (*throughout punches*) Wives submit yourselves unto your
husband as unto the Lord! Wives submit yourselves
unto your husband as unto the Lord!!!

(*He pulls away, starts pacing, shaking his hand in
pain.* **WILLI** *rises, blood streaming from her mouth and
nose, crying, making painful, animalistic sounds. She
stumbles, retreats to the opposite side of the sofa as* **J.D.**
*opens the refrigerator and grabs a beer, opens it, tosses
the cap in the sink and starts swigging.* **WILLI** *stumbles
to the bookshelf, steadies herself against it, back to audience. She grabs a tissue, wipes her mouth and discreetly
takes the gun from behind the Bible, bends over in pain,
hiding the gun between both hands, in her skirt. She circles the couch, stands back to the audience facing* **J.D.**)

It all started when you broke my TV. That's when it all
started. You drove me to this. I told you not to get a
job, and I didn't even get to finish my lunch. I love you
so much, Willi and I want you to do what the Bible says
so we can be happy.

(*He throws the beer bottle in the sink and starts down
the hall.*)

**WILLI.** J.D.?

(*He turns.*)

I am so sorry.

(*Then she raises the gun and pulls the trigger. BAM,
BAM, BAM, BAM.* **J.D.** *slumps over, falls into the hallway. PIANO MUSIC as* **WILLI** *just stands there, staring.
She begins sobbing as she goes and places the gun on the
counter, grabs a pot holder and frantically takes out all
her precious items from the oven. She finds the pictures
of the kids.*)

My babies. My babies.

(*She stumbles over to* **J.D.**'s *chair, holding everything.*)

**LA SONIA.** *(O.S.)* Willi. Willi. Oh, Willi, please –

*(LA SONIA rushes in, takes it all in, sees J.D.'s body.)*

*(mutters)* Oh my God.

*(The BLUES SINGER, in silhouette, appears in the wings and sings slowly and soulfully. She wears a red hat along with the red church dress which tells us that she is the ghost of LA SONIA's baby sister. She reprises "If You Believe, You Can Achieve.")*

**BLUES SINGER.**

Even in your darkest hour…

**WILLI.** I am not gonna shrivel up and die.

**BLUES SINGER.**

Keep the faith.

You have the power.

**LA SONIA.** No, Willi baby, we ain't gonna let that happen to ya.

*(She kneels beside WILLI, comforting her.)*

**BLUES SINGER.**

Anything is possible

If You…

Lord, If You

Just Believe!

*(BLACKOUT)*

**The End**

# PROPS PLOT

**Preset Willi's Trailer**
*Living area*
TV remote
Dictionary
Screw driver
Pliers
Hammer
Bible
Kleenex

*Kitchen*
Popcorn bowl
Timer
Plates
Cups
Silverware
Napkins
Recipe Box – photos of children inside
Skillet
Metal bowl
Pyrex dish
Coffee mug
Pot holder

*Food*
Pot on stovetop with green beans in it
Bag of almost empty Lay's potato chips on counter with chip clip
Coffee maker with coffee
Cookie jar with cookies
Loaf of Wonder Bread
Bag of popcorn – popped – pre-set in microwave
Bag of popcorn – not popped

*Fridge*
Pitcher full of tea
Bottled beer
Can of condensed milk
Tuna casserole *Note – original production used white cheddar mac and cheese precooked

*Preset Spotlight Bar*
Bottled beer
Red plastic snack baskets
Wax paper
Bar snacks
Ashtrays

Cigarettes
Puzzle book
Bag of Frito's
Bar towel
Broom
Dust pan

## Preset Offstage

*Act I*
Case of beer
O Magazine
Metal lunchbox
Wal-Mart grocery bag:
Can of peach halves
Cool Whip

*Act II*
Metal lunch box
Small portable TV
Empty Pyrex dish
Internet research papers
Wal-Mart grocery bag:
Box of cake mix
Canned crushed pineapples
Canned cherry pie filling
Steak
Dr. Phil paperback book
Newspaper want ads

## Preset Offstage

*Act III*
Wal-Mart vest with smiley face stickers in the pocket
Wal-Mart nametag

## Additional Notes

1) All cans to be opened onstage should be pull tab
2) Original production used a fake cherry dump delight preset in the oven for Willi to throw in the trash at the end of Act II, leaving the dish full of real ingredients in the oven
3) Important note on gun usage – the original production used a dummy prop gun for JD to use with LaSonia and Rayleen. After he set it on the bookshelf, Willi switched to a live gun to fire empty load blanks. At no point should JD be directing a gun that is capable of firing ammunition of any kind near the actresses' heads.

# COSTUME PLOT

**THE BLUES SINGER**
*"Trials & Tribulations" number*
Long red beaded/sequined evening gown featuring haltered neck with thigh-high slit on the side
Red heels
Ruby earrings
Ruby wedding band

*"Ode to Womankind" number*
Form-fitting red "flapper dress"
20's era red pumps
Dangly red earrings
Ruby wedding band

*"Waiting Game" number*
Long red evening gown w/beaded bodice & halter neck featuring flowing floor-length chiffon skirt
Red heels
Large matching red "Billie Holiday" flower (pinned in hair)
Ruby earrings
Ruby wedding band

*"If You Believe You Can Achieve" number*
Form-fitting bright red church suit, featuring ruffled lapel and cuffs; above-the-knee skirt
Red heels
Ruby earrings
Ruby wedding band
(add matching wide-brim red church hat for the reprise/finalé)

**WILLADEAN "WILLI" WINKLER**
*Act One*
Light blue, sleeveless cotton top
Black and blue subdued floral print skirt (¾ length)
Cream colored sandals
Silver wedding band

*Act Two*
Pale pink, sleeveless cotton top
Subdued floral print skirt with pink & tan accents (¾ length)
Cream colored sandals
Silver wedding band

*Act Three*
Long sleeve peach colored blouse (multiples recommended)
Knee-length khaki wrap-around shirt with deep pockets (multiples recommended)
Wal-Mart smock (with "Willadean" nametag)
Navy flats/low-heeled shoes
Silver wedding band

**J.D. WINKLER**
The following ensemble is worn throughout, with slight variations (mid-scene lose ball cap, workshirt, etc.)
Short sleeve navy/dark-colored workshirt with sewn-on "JD" nametag
White "wife beater" tank
Worn blue jeans
Black workboots
Black leather belt
Silver wedding band
Black "Dallas Cowboys" ball cap

**RAYLEEN HOBBS**
*Act One*
Skimpy orange halter top with bare midriff
Strapless push-up bra
"Too-tight" denim mini-skirt
Dangly earrings
Zebra print, open-toe high heels

*Act Two*
Skin-tight tie-dye tank
Cut-off denim short-shorts ("Daisy Dukes")
Zebra print, open-toe high heels
Quick-change for "Waiting Game" number
Tight yellow tank
Busy floral print push-up bra (shows underneath tank)
Same denim skirt
Same earrings
Same zebra print, open-toe high heels

*Act Three*
Pale green tube-top (no bra)
Cut-off denim short-shorts ("Daisy Dukes")
Bright orange, scuffed platform stilettos
Green bandana/handkerchief

**LA SONIA ROBINSON**
*Act One*
Pink V-neck T-shirt
Gray sweat pants
House slippers
"Heart" necklace
Wristwatch
Gold wedding band

*Act Two*

Black and blue flannel/western shirt with snaps (sleeves cuffed at elbow)
Gray sweat pants
House slippers
"Heart" necklace
Wristwatch
Gold wedding band
Sexy black negligee (hidden underneath flannel shirt and sweats)

*Act Three*
Pale blue V-neck T-shirt
Dark blue sweat pants
House slippers
"Heart" necklace
Wristwatch
Gold Wedding band

**THE PIANO PLAYER**
Black suit
Red Oxford shirt
Black tie
Black loafers
Black fedora (with red trim)

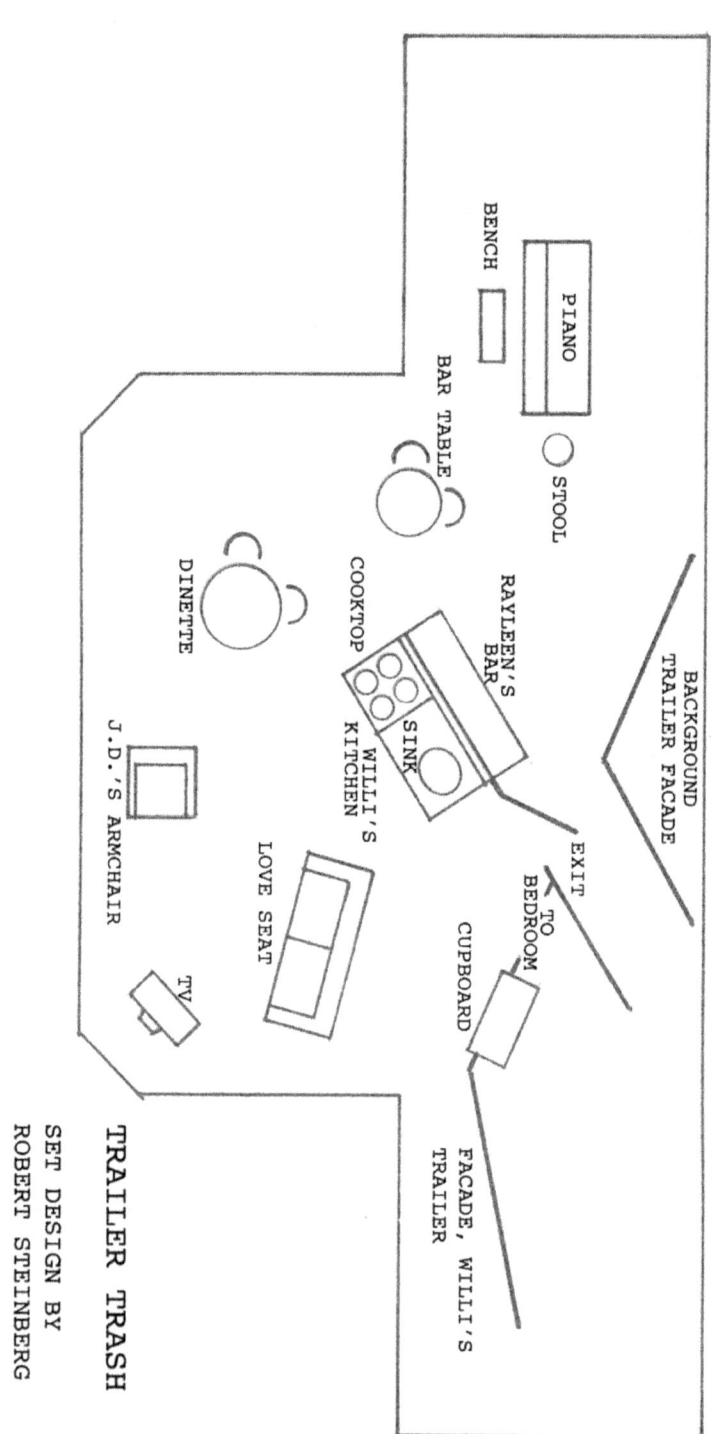

TRAILER TRASH

SET DESIGN BY
ROBERT STEINBERG

Also by
# Del Shores...

## Cheatin'
## Daddy's Dyin' (Who's Got the Will?)
## Daughters of the Lone Star State
## Sordid Lives
## Southern Baptist Sissies

Please visit our website **samuelfrench.com** for complete
descriptions and licensing information

Reviews of and Accolades for
# THE TRIALS AND TRIBULATIONS OF A TRAILER TRASH HOUSEWIFE...

"A feat of breathtaking audacity."
Critics Choice
*- Los Angeles Times*

"Shores manages to fully explore Willadean's horrific plight while infusing the work with such hilarity the audience is often reduced to tears and laughter within the same breath."
*- Daily Variety*

In 2003, *The Trials and Tribulations of a Trailer Trash Housewife* was the winner of more than 14 **Los Angeles Theatre Awards**, including Best Production, Best Lead Performance – Beth Grant, and Best World Premiere from the Los Angeles Drama Critics Circle; Best Lead Actress – Beth Grant from the **Ovation Awards**; Best Production and Best Playwright from the **NAACP Theatre Awards**; Best Production, Best Playwright, Best Direction, Best Lead Performance – Beth Grant, and Best Supporting Performance – Dale Dickey, from the **Back Stage West Garland Awards**; and Best Playwright, Best Supporting Actor – David Steen, Best Ensemble – Beth Grant, Dale Dickey, Debby Holiday, Octavia Spencer, David Steen, from the **L.A. Weekly Awards**.

# OTHER TITLES AVAILABLE FROM SAMUEL FRENCH

## GUTENBERG! THE MUSICAL!
### Scott Brown and Anthony King

*2m / Musical Comedy*

In this two-man musical spoof, a pair of aspiring playwrights perform a backers' audition for their new project - a big, splashy musical about printing press inventor Johann Gutenberg. With an unending supply of enthusiasm, Bud and Doug sing all the songs and play all the parts in their crass historical epic, with the hope that one of the producers in attendance will give them a Broadway contract – fulfilling their ill-advised dreams.

"A smashing success!"
*- The New York Times*

"Brilliantly realized and side-splitting!
*- New York Magazine*

"There are lots of genuine laughs in Gutenberg!"
*- New York Post*

www.ingramcontent.com/pod-product-compliance
Lightning Source LLC
Chambersburg PA
CBHW070647120726
47909CB00004B/1613